Further Praise for *The Last Days of California*

Barnes & Noble Discover Pick
Indie Next Pick

"[A] terrific first novel. . . . *The Last Days of California* joins a number of other recent novels written from the perspective of children or teenagers—Karen Thompson Walker's *The Age of Miracles*, Lauren Groff's *Arcadia*. It's hard to figure out why some are published as 'young adult' while others aren't, but why worry about labeling a book this good? Just read it."   —Laurie Muchnick,
New York Times Book Review

"Miller's prose bestows a magnetic beauty on gas-station bathroom stops, Waffle House lunches, and the cast of overfed, overstimulated travelers the Metcalfs encounter along the interstates. . . . [She delivers] raw the heartbreaking futility of the Metcalfs' small triumphs, private embarrassments, and poor decisions with such hilarious precision that you become completely involved in their struggles—and, ultimately, in awe of their abiding hope."   —Catherine Straut, *Elle*

"Like a map that, despite its well-worn creases, is impossible to refold, the trip doesn't wind up where you think it will, nor do the characters. And Miller's novel is better for it."   —Laura Pearson,
Chicago Tribune

"Mary Miller's *The Last Days of California* is hilarious and heartbreaking, dark and beautiful, a novel written by one of the most observant and mordant writers alive. Miller (as the many fans of her short stories already know) knows how to write about the restless heart of the trapped. This book is terrific."

—Elizabeth McCracken, author of
An Exact Replica of a Figment of My Imagination
and *The Giant's House*

"*The Last Days of California* is a literary snapshot of our times that portrays the affirmation and doubt we often find in family and faith. This coming-of-age story of a young girl whose family is on a cross-country trip to witness Armageddon is, at its core, the story of this country's push and pull with popular culture, religious zealotry, and the human element that drives both. Like our heroine, Jess, asks of herself, *The Last Days of California* implores the reader to consider two very basic questions: 'Who are we, and who do we want to be?'"

—Wiley Cash, *New York Times* best-selling author of
This Dark Road to Mercy and *A Land More Kind Than Home*

"A humane, funny, and genuinely unsettling coming-of-age story that falls somewhere between the tales of Flannery O'Connor and Terrence Malick's film *Badlands*. . . . *The Last Days of California* not only transcends its predecessor, but beats most debuts by a Texas mile. Even if the Metcalfs don't make it to heaven, Miller's readers have no choice but to ascend."   —Eugenia Williamson,
Boston Globe

"A beautiful examination of youth and family and what it means to be alive (and to fear dying) in contemporary America. . . . Rarely, if ever, have we seen young American womanhood painted in such a raw and honest and heartbreaking way. . . . Miller's writing is all we need to carry us. Like Willy Vlautin, she can drive a nail into your heart with the simple sadnesses of being alive and being afraid."

—William Boyle, *Los Angeles Review of Books*

"Spot-on, hilarious, and ultra-relatable. . . . [S]ometimes a road-trip novel, particularly one as compulsively devourable as *The Last Days of California*, is just what you need to get that elusively giddy, hopeful feeling back."

—Hannah Hickok, *Redbook*

"Breezy, colloquial, with little or no flourish to her speech, Jess . . . proves acerbic, straightforward, awkward, afraid and strangely charming."

—Josh Cook, *Minneapolis Star Tribune*

"With a perfect blend of anxiety-tinged wonderment and adventure-seeking hormones, Miller . . . gives voice to Jess's teenage ambivalence about growing up and being saved."

—Megan O'Grady, Vogue.com

"On a family road trip to witness the rapture, fifteen-year-old Jess learns that the only person she's going to save is herself. *The Last Days of California* is an affecting coming-of-age story from an inspired new voice."

—Elliott Holt, author of *You Are One of Them*

"Go on this road trip with Miller's heroine, Jess. You couldn't ask for a better companion across a country and a family's wastelands. Through Jess, Miller manages wisdom without cynicism, creates a teenager with grace and warmth and lessons to share for burnt-out adults bored of irony. Get in the car and roll through the great questions about how to have faith in god or family or country, get in the car and become a believer." —Tupelo Hassman, author of *Girlchild*

"Miller gives an accurate portrayal of teenage angst with seamless and beautiful prose." —Emily Gatlin, *Clarion-Ledger*

"The debut of a promising new voice, a voice that describes the painful longing for transcendence and connectedness with compelling vividness and candor." —Emily Colette Wilkinson,
Weekly Standard

"Brimming with acute observation and inspired prose, Mary Miller's *The Last Days of California* is a blessing of a book." —Stevie Godson, *New York Journal of Books*

"Miller's depiction of family dynamics is stunning. . . . The author has created a haunting, unforgettable atmosphere by combining the boredom and intimacy of riding in a car all day as a family, enervated by the coming end of the world. Jess's perfect narrative voice captures a young teen's uncertainty." —Angela Carstensen,
School Library Journal

"*The Last Days of California* is the *Sense and Sensibility* of preapocalypse America, and Jess and Elise may be my new favorite literary sisters: different as night and day, on a road trip to the rapture with their evangelical parents, they find they have nothing to lose but each other. Mary Miller is a ventriloquist of adolescent angst and a nervy surveyor of American culture."   —Alexis Smith, author of *Glaciers*

"*The Last Days of California* is a road novel reinvented for our apocalypse-obsessed age, a coming-of-age story so precisely insightful about our contemporary life that it seems as if it could only have been written from the future. If the rapture comes, I'll gladly be left behind if it means getting to read more books by the extraordinary Mary Miller: She possesses one of the boldest new voices in fiction, a speech born out of the South but that aims to speak for all of America—and succeeds."   —Matt Bell, author of *In the House upon the Dirt between the Lake and the Woods*

"*The Last Days of California* reads like a dream you're having on a restless night. What seems bizarre when viewed from the outside looks like plain old fallible life from the inside. . . . Isn't it marvelous that Mary Miller could leave me twisting in the wind that way?"   — Dennis Haritou, Three Guys One Book

"Mary Miller's debut novel will move, will impress, will leave even some small part of the reader rearranged, in the way that her four characters are becoming decisively different over the course of this novel."   —Vincent Scarpa, *American Short Fiction*

"A triumphant addition to the long tradition of coming-of-age stories, showing us that even those who seem to be nothing like us—be they ballerinas, superheroes, or teenage daughters of fundamentalist

Christians—they really are more like us than we know. . . There is a great pleasure in recognizing yourself in a book as beautifully written as this." —Joseph Riippi, Electric Literature

"Reveling in the dysfunction of its characters, *The Last Days of California* is no fairy tale, but it is timely, true and—at times—even a little bit tender. Miller is a talent to watch." —Stephenie Harrison, *BookPage*

"*The Last Days of California* is a book worth evangelizing for. Miller takes the reader on an eye-opening road trip through adolescent insecurities, fast food restaurants, and sexual awakening. It's a coming-of-age novel for the faithful and the faithless—and anyone in between." —Michele Filgate, writer and events coordinator at Community Bookstore, Brooklyn, New York

"Sending up religious extremism in deadpan prose, Miller makes this coming-of-age tale work as both a poignant portrait of a bright but vulnerable teen and a biting social critique. Supersmart fiction from an arresting new talent." —Joanne Wilkinson, *Booklist*, starred review

"[A]n incredibly wry and fresh take on the coming-of-age novel with Jess at its center. . . . It's impossible not to root for Jess—as it was with June in *Tell the Wolves I'm Home* or Bee in *Where'd You Go, Bernadette*? It's impossible not to fall in love with *The Last Days of California*." —Miwa Messer, *Everyday Ebook*

"Beyond the well-crafted coming-of-age narrative, Miller gets every little detail about the South—from the way the sky greens before a storm to gas stations where Hank Williams Jr.'s 'Family Tradition' blares—just right. . . . In Jess, Miller has created a narrator worthy of comparison with those of contemporaries such as Karen Thompson Walker and of greats such as Carson McCullers."

—*Publishers Weekly*, starred review

"In capturing the particular anxieties of a teenage girl, Miller is capturing some of the universal anxieties of any age, and she does so with the kind of empathy and curiosity about the world that is sorely needed in American thought." — Zach VandeZande, American Microreviews and Interviews

"A brave book with extraordinary prose and vulnerable characters that grow beyond their immediate experiences and become—like Waffle House and the many fast food restaurants—almost universal."

—Sam Price, *Heavy Feather Review*

THE
LAST
DAYS OF
CALIFORNIA

LIVERIGHT PUBLISHING CORPORATION

A Division of W. W. Norton & Company

New York / *London*

THE
LAST
DAYS OF
CALIFORNIA

A NOVEL

Mary Miller

For information about permission to reproduce selections from this book,
write to Permissions, Liveright Publishing Corporation,
a division of W. W. Norton & Company, Inc.,
500 Fifth Avenue, New York, NY 10110

For information about special discounts for bulk purchases,
please contact W. W. Norton Special Sales
at specialsales@wwnorton.com or 800-233-4830

Manufacturing by Courier Westford
Book design by Ellen Cipriano
Production manager: Julia Druskin

Library of Congress Cataloging-in-Publication Data

Miller, Mary, 1977–
The Last Days of California : a novel / Mary Miller. — First edition.
pages cm
ISBN 978-0-87140-588-3 (hardcover)
1. Teenage girls—Fiction. 2. Families—Religious life—Fiction. 3. Rapture
(Christian eschatology)—Fiction. 4. Christians—Fiction. 5. Road fiction. I. Title.
PS3613.I5446L37 2014
813'.6—dc23

2013039350

ISBN 978-0-87140-841-9 pbk.

Liveright Publishing Corporation
500 Fifth Avenue, New York, N.Y. 10110
www.wwnorton.com

W. W. Norton & Company Ltd.
Castle House, 75/76 Wells Street, London W1T 3QT

1 2 3 4 5 6 7 8 9 0

For my parents,
Dolores and Curt

THE
LAST
DAYS OF
CALIFORNIA

WEDNESDAY

It was Wednesday and we hadn't even made it to Texas yet. We'd been sleeping late, swimming during daylight hours, but we were going to have to move if we wanted to make it to California in time.

In a shitty little town in Louisiana, which was full of shitty little towns, we stopped at a Waffle House and sat at the counter. My father liked to sit at counters because he liked to be among the people—you couldn't just ask if they'd been saved, you had to win them over first, had to make them like you—but there was no time left for niceties. He had brought along a bundle of tracts that said "All Suffering SOON TO END!"

When the waitress asked how we were doing, he handed her one.

"The world is passing away," he said, "but those who do the will of God will remain forever."

In response, she set a tiny napkin in front of him with a

knife and fork on top. Then she moved down the line: my sister, Elise, and my mother and me.

I watched my father, who was looking around pleasantly to see if there was anyone who might be willing to talk to him. There wasn't. There hardly ever was. He was either preaching to the choir or trying to convert the unconvertible, but it didn't stop him from going through the motions—the futility of it was central, necessary. He didn't really want all 7 billion people on the planet to be saved. We wouldn't be special then. We wouldn't be the chosen ones.

I set my elbows on the counter. It was sticky with syrup, and I liked that this Waffle House was like every other Waffle House I'd ever been to. I knew where the bathroom was and what I wanted to eat and what it would taste like.

I peeled my elbows off the counter and looked at them.

"Excuse me, miss," my mother said, too quietly for the waitress to hear her. "Excuse me," she said again, louder.

The waitress came over and stood in front of us. She was tall and hulking and had a missing tooth, or maybe it was just a large gap—the space didn't seem quite big enough for a tooth. I stared at her openly. She was ugly and I wasn't afraid of ugly people.

"This counter is sticky," my mother said, touching it with her finger.

The waitress left and came back, wiped it off with a dirty-looking rag.

Elise dug around in her purse and pulled out her lip gloss. She smeared it on her bottom lip and top lip and pressed them together. It was almost obscene, watching her put on makeup.

Boys frequently told me she was a knockout and then waited expectantly for my response. Of course there was nothing to do but agree. She was a knockout and I wasn't. What was there to say about it?

"Why don't y'all go clean up?" our mother asked. Neither Elise nor I said anything. We didn't respond to suggestions, only direct orders.

I brought my hands to my face. "Clean as a whistle," I said.

"I wonder where that saying comes from," my sister said. "Whistles aren't clean, they're full of spit." She got out her phone and Googled it, and I watched her face as she read, the dents at the tops of her eyebrows. "'One possibility is that the old simile describes the whistling sound of a sword as it swishes through the air to decapitate someone, and an early nineteenth-century quotation suggests this connection: a first-rate shot, his head taken off as clean as a whistle.'"

She hopped off her stool and I turned to watch her go, ponytail and hips swinging. It was how she walked down the halls of our high school. She never looked at anybody and made people call her name again and again before turning. She was wearing her King Jesus Returns! t-shirt with a pair of shorts that were so short you couldn't tell she was wearing them. I saw a man watching her, too, a mean-looking little man with a girl on his lap. The girl was skinny with big joints and glasses, one arm choking a ratty stuffed animal. He pulled her thumb out of her mouth and she put it back and he pulled it out and she put it back in again. I looked around at the other diners: they were all hideous. I could live easily in a town like this.

The man's food came and he scooted the girl off of his lap and dug in. She reached for a triangle of toast and he slapped her hand.

"Ask first," he said, but she didn't ask and he didn't give it to her. I imagined a scenario in which the girl had been kidnapped years ago. She'd been with him so long that she had forgotten any other life ever existed.

My mother reached over me to get a packet of Sweet'n Low and I leaned back in an exaggerated manner. She smelled bad, like a wounded animal. She had gotten her period as soon as we'd left Montgomery, and it reminded me that I hadn't showered in days. I'd gone swimming last night, though, had stayed in the pool for hours listening to Elise talk to a boy who was selling magazines across the country. Every morning, the boy woke up early and drove to a different town. He didn't have time to see anything or do anything and he ate fast food off dollar menus to save money. He wanted to go home, but he had barely made anything after his expenses—he might even end up owing *them*. It was modern-day indentured servitude, he'd said. I'd been waiting for Elise to one-up him with her pregnancy, or to tell him that our father was driving us twenty-five hundred miles so that we would be among the last people in the Continental U.S. to witness the coming of Our Savior, the Lord Jesus Christ, but she didn't say anything except that we were going to see the Pacific Ocean.

Elise sat back down and poured two creamers into her coffee, stirred it with a fork. She drank coffee every morning now; she'd drink cup after cup and hold up her hand so I could watch it shake.

When the waitress returned, my father ordered a T-bone and my sister ordered a waffle and my mother ordered a Fiesta Omelet and I ordered a hamburger. Elise had stopped eating meat six months ago, but I'd catch her stealing glances at our pulled pork sandwiches, our sausage-filled side of the pizza. She had a whole spiel about animal rights and the environment and the nutritional requirements of the human body and our father had his own spiel—he said if people stopped eating meat, animals would overrun our cities and wreak havoc and the economy would crash. He said if meat weren't available, people would turn to cannibalism.

My father searched his pockets and went outside, came back and divvied up a thin newspaper. He handed me the entertainment section, and I read my horoscope and checked to see what was coming on TV later. I hoped my sister and I would have our own room again so we could watch whatever we wanted.

"*Honey, I Shrunk the Kids* is on at eight," I said, leaning over my mother to show Elise. We loved movies from the 1980s, the ridiculous clothes and graphics, the clunky phones and boom boxes. We liked *The Last Starfighter, Sixteen Candles, The Goonies.* We liked anything with Andrew McCarthy and Judd Nelson, who were so old now. If they were raptured, they'd be restored to their former beauty. I liked Andrew McCarthy best in *Less Than Zero*, Judd Nelson in *The Breakfast Club.* Molly Ringwald was never pretty enough to be a leading lady, but the eighties were a dream world in which the captain of the football team would leave the homecoming queen for an awkward red-haired girl who made her own clothes.

I watched the cook break my patty off a stack and place it on the grill. He seasoned the steak and cracked eggs into a bowl, moving so fast he seemed to be doing all of these things at once. He wore a little paper hat to distinguish himself. It was a nice touch, old-timey. I picked up the entertainment section again and read Elise's horoscope. I wanted to tell her what it said, but our parents thought horoscopes were evil because the only one who knew what was going to happen was God. Elise's advised against extended travel, which she would have found amusing. Mine said I was on an information-gathering mission of sorts— I was to keep my questions unstructured and people were going to tell me the most unusual facts about themselves and the world. I liked the sound of this, particularly the "of sorts" part. My mission could be whatever I wanted.

I passed Elise the entertainment section and my father passed me the front page and my mother was stuck with the sports. Like all mothers everywhere, she had no use for sports. I read about the drought in Louisiana. We were passing through a red zone labeled "exceptional drought."

"I think the end times have already begun," I said, showing them a picture of a woman standing on the ashes of her house. She had her face in her hands, a couple of smudged children in the background.

"This is nothing compared to what's coming," our father said. "It'll be like nothing we could even imagine. There'll be three 9/11s in a day—tornadoes in places that have never seen tornadoes and earthquakes where there are no fault lines. The sun'll turn red as blood and bodies'll be piled up everywhere.

Thank God we won't be around to see it." He always sounded so excited when he talked about the tribulations. He liked the idea of all the sinners getting what was coming to them while we were rewarded with eternal life.

"These things have always happened," Elise said, pouring another creamer into her coffee.

"They seem to be happening a lot more now," I said.

"They're just reporting on them more, or they come in cycles we're too young to remember," she said. "I'll tweet Anderson Cooper for some hard stats, it's probably just global warming."

"It seems like everything's global warming." I wasn't sure what global warming was, exactly, but it felt disappointing. Our father didn't believe in it. He said it had been made up by the Left for political gain. I could see him wanting to say something, but our food came and he picked up his napkin and set it on one knee. Then we all bowed our heads.

"Thank you, Lord," he said. I kept my eyes open and watched the cook's legs move, the slight bulge in his pants. "These are simple words, but they come from simple hearts that overflow with the realization of your goodness. We ask you to bless us as we eat, bless this food and bless the hands that prepared it. May the words of our lips spring forth from hearts of gratitude and may we bless others as we fellowship today."

As soon as he said "Amen," Elise was typing on her phone, thumbs moving fast over the keyboard. She stopped and reread it to herself before reading it aloud so I could tell her it sounded good. She loved Anderson Cooper, thought of him as a personal friend. He was gay, though—never before had there been so many homosexuals: *"If a man also lie with mankind, they shall surely be put to death; their blood shall be upon them."*

While the rest of us ate, Elise drank coffee and paged through the paper. She checked her fingers to see if they were ink-smudged, picked up her phone and set it back down. She was about to cut into her waffle when her phone signaled the arrival of a text message. She smiled and shook her head, so it must have been Dan, the boy who had done this to her, only he didn't know it yet, and maybe never would. She wasn't like the girls from *16 and Pregnant* whose boyfriends left them to raise the baby alone, frazzled and post-baby fat, studying for the GED.

When the last of my burger began to fall apart, I pushed my plate away.

"Do you want my waffle?" Elise asked.

"Okay," I said.

"You aren't going to eat anything?" our father asked. He didn't like it when we didn't eat. It made him angry.

"I'm not hungry," she said.

"You need to eat something. You hardly had any dinner last night."

She slid her plate over to me and I scraped butter into the holes, filled them with syrup. Elise was sick with the baby and the driving and she'd always had a weak stomach, like our father. She was the delicate sister, she liked to tell me, which wasn't true, but I'd found there was no use in telling people what they were like.

The waitress wedged the check between the napkin holder

and saltshaker and my father picked it up and went over it carefully, running his finger down the column. He had a number 3
in black ink on the back of his right hand. Every morning he
scrubbed it clean and wrote a new number—tomorrow would
be 2 and then 1 and then 0. At zero, we would be in California,
listening to the rapture on the radio or watching it on TV. I still
didn't understand why he thought it was important for us to be
among the last; it was something he had gotten into his head.

Elise took the check from him and looked it over. "It's right,
Dad," she said.

He paid with cash, counting out the bills carefully and probably leaving a bad tip, and led me to the door with a warm hand
on my back. "My girl," he said, patting. Whenever he put a hand
on my body, it went up and down and up and down like it was
difficult for him to touch me for more than a second at a time.

———————

In the trees, birds made sounds like dogs whimpering. They
flew down to pick through a patch of fresh dirt.

"What are those?" I asked.

"White-winged doves," he said.

"Like the kind you hunt?"

"Cousins."

"They sure are fat," I said, looking up at him, my eyes landing momentarily on the sun. He hunted doves every fall, brought
them home by the sack for our mother to soak in Wish-Bone
and wrap in bacon, and I was always scared I was going to bite
into a pellet but I never did.

My father unlocked the Taurus and we got in. He was about to back up when he noticed the rearview mirror had fallen off. Our mother picked it up off the floorboard and handed it to him without comment. She had become suddenly, suspiciously quiet. I didn't know what was going on with her. I hadn't asked. She took her clip-on sunglasses out of the glove box and cleaned them with her shirt. They were blue-tinted and held onto her regular glasses by a magnet.

My father swore as he tried to stick the mirror back on, and then he handed it to my mother and started backing up.

"Is there anything behind me?" he asked, already out of the parking spot.

Elise and I collected wrappers and bottles and handed them up to our mother, stacked the magazines and placed them on the hump between us. Elise moved the bag of snacks to her side of the floorboard. It was full of things we'd never buy at home: Cheddar & Bacon Potato Skins, peanut butter wrapped in pretzels, squares of fudge that appeared homemade but had probably been made in a factory like everything else. I wasn't going to look in the bag because I was sure the fudge had leaked out of its plastic and made a mess of everything. I liked having these snacks—they felt like protection against something. I could conjure up all sorts of scenarios in which they might save our lives.

Our father rolled to a stop at a red light, and I watched a one-legged woman hobble down the concrete median. She was slim and youngish with shoulder-length hair and a sign that said ON MY LAST LEG. I socked Elise in the arm and she pulled a twenty-dollar bill out of her purse and handed it to me. I pushed the button on the door; my window went down, stopping not even halfway.

"What are you doing?" my father asked. He didn't like it when anybody rolled down the window. He hit the door-lock button.

"We're giving the woman some money," Elise said.

"She'll just use it to buy drugs," he said.

"It's possible."

"There are services for homeless people," my mother said. "They don't have to stand out here in the heat all day begging." She looked at my father and I studied her profile. My mother was a plain woman who didn't do much in the way of improving herself. She wore very little makeup and black or khaki pants with oversized shirts. She dyed her hair, but only the flat medium brown that was her usual shade, which she hid from my father as if he wouldn't be able to go on loving her if he found out. She reminded me of Marcie from *Peanuts*, compact and nondescript with round glasses that hid her eyes. I wanted her to be more like some of my friends' mothers, who wore jewelry and nice dresses with heels; even the fat ones seemed regal, proud.

"Give her a tract, Jess," my father said, his arm swinging back and forth at my legs. He got a weak hold on my ankle and I yanked it away.

The woman hobbled over on her crutch and took the bill.

"God bless you," she said, shoving it into the good-leg pocket of her jeans. It reminded me of the times homeless people had said this to me when I hadn't given them anything, how nasty it could sound. The woman looked almost normal close-up, her face dry and brown but pretty.

My father cracked his window. "It doesn't take God any time at all to save someone," he said. "In the last hour of a terribly sinful life, the thief on the cross was saved by Christ." She gave him the finger. The car behind us honked.

"Go," my mother said, leaning forward.

My father stepped on the gas and the car jerked into motion. He viewed the bad reactions as a spiritual test. Otherwise, he wouldn't compare a woman he didn't know to the thief on the cross, he wouldn't be such an asshole. He followed the line of cars merging onto the interstate and I wondered if anyone missed the woman and wanted her to come home. I didn't know how people survived if there was no one to miss them.

"'And he said unto Jesus, Lord, remember me when thou comest into thy kingdom,'" our father continued. "'And Jesus said unto him, verily I say unto thee, today thou shalt be with me in paradise.'" He repeated "paradise." In paradise, he wouldn't have to work or worry about money. In paradise, he wouldn't have to take insulin shots, pinching the fat on his stomach and stabbing himself before meals. Half the time he didn't do it and we didn't remind him. He had an Asian doctor he called Woo who always sent him home with pamphlets about diet and exercise, which only pissed him off—he ate more ice cream and drank more Coke now than ever. He had also started drinking alcohol, which wasn't something he would have ever done before. It seemed to represent a terrible shift: a complete resignation, all hell breaking loose.

Ten minutes later, he was still thinking about Elise's dona-tion to the one-legged woman. "How much did you give her?" he asked.

"A fiver," Elise said. She flipped a page in her magazine, stop-ping to look at a woman lying on a floor in a matching bra-and-panty set, her rib bones sticking out severely. The woman was reading a book, advertising glasses.

"That's a lot of money," he said.

"She needs it more than we do, and her sign was funny."

"It wasn't funny," I said, "it was sad."

"You have no sense of humor."

"I have a sense of humor," I said, but I thought about it and decided that my sense of humor probably wasn't very good. Peo-ple had to explain jokes to me and I'd say they weren't funny and the person would say of course they weren't funny—you had to get them right away for them to be funny. I didn't understand that, either, how getting them right away made them funny.

I watched the mile markers pass and then picked up one of Elise's magazines. I liked them because they arrived in the mail full of slick colorful ads, smelling like perfume, and they told you how to do everything without even trying. I left it open on my lap and looked out the window again. Interstate miles were boring, though the font on the signs changed by state and some-times it was hilly before it was flat again. I watched for Starbucks and Love's gas stations. Starbucks had the chocolate graham crackers I liked, and Love's had a good selection of baked goods and ripe bananas. I saw a sign for Chick-fil-A and wondered why I only wanted it on Sunday, when it was closed.

I readjusted my seatbelt and propped my feet on the tracts. We had passed out dozens of them, but the bundle didn't seem to be getting any smaller and I wanted to throw them out the window: they'd get stuck in the branches of trees; prisoners would stab them with their pokers. I picked up one—the picture garish, Technicolor—a man and a woman sitting in a field surrounded by cows and horses and chickens. There were barrels of apples and pumpkins in the foreground. In the background, a nice house and lots of trees and a blue, blue sky. In a nod to multiculturalism, the man and woman could have been Mexican or Middle Eastern or Native American. I reread it for the thousandth time: God made Adam and Eve perfect, but He didn't want them to be mindless robots so He gave them free will, which they used to disobey Him. As a result, God was letting us see how poorly we were able to rule ourselves by allowing this experiment with total freedom to continue, but it would soon come to an end because we'd messed it up big time— thousands of years of war and poverty and suffering.

I thought about it, God holding us accountable for something we hadn't done and then letting us continue to rule ourselves so badly for so long in order to show us that we needed Him. I hadn't ever thought about it before, really. The logic seemed sketchy.

I had handed out these tracts in shopping malls, left them between the pages of books in libraries and bookstores. I'd handed them out at parades and street festivals and I'd once gone door-to-door with an older boy from church but our pastor said door-to-door wasn't our territory—we weren't Jehovah's

Witnesses, we weren't LDS. For all my time and efforts, I hadn't saved a single person. Even the believers didn't want to talk to me. They wanted to shop for blue jeans and summer reading books in peace.

————

Elise rested her head on my shoulder, and I smelled mint from whatever shampoo she'd used this morning. Then she took her makeup bag out of her purse and spread the bottles and containers around. I wanted to touch them, smell them. I loved going through her things. "Would you hold the mirror?" she asked.

I tried to hold it steady as she put on her base coat. She applied blush, eye shadow, eyeliner, and mascara, stopping every once and a while to adjust my hand or tell me I was holding it too low.

"I can't believe you wear all that stuff. Doesn't it feel like your face is melting off?"

"It makes me feel pretty," she said, screwing the tops back on and putting everything away. "You want to play poker?"

"Not really," I said, but she took the deck of cards out anyhow, shuffled them on one knee. A few fell to the floor. I counted out pistachio shells because we weren't allowed to gamble with real money, not even pennies. Sometimes we gambled with the good bobby pins we were always swiping from each other, the ones you could only find at Sally's, but we were running low.

I had a crap hand—2 of clubs, 10 of clubs, 6 of hearts. I put mine down and she put hers down, but then she picked hers back up and checked them again. She wasn't good at cards, wasn't good at games in general, but it didn't make her not want to play.

A motorcycle gang roared past and we stopped to watch them go by, only one with a woman on the back, her long hair whipping itself into knots. I imagined the woman Indian-style on a bed, combing out her wet hair, and then I imagined the man combing it for her. He would tell her how beautiful she was even though she was old and had eye bags, even though her stomach was flabby from having his children. I wanted to sit on a bed with a man who would comb out my hair and tell me I was beautiful. No one ever told me this except for very old women who thought all young people were beautiful.

After the motorcycles passed, I spotted something large and headless in the road, a swath of bright red like a can of spilled paint. There were scavengers circling above, waiting for a lull in traffic so they could swoop down. Their shadows on the pavement were all wingspan.

I popped a pistachio shell into my mouth. It was still salty. I picked up another and another and tossed them in.

"Think of all the things those have touched," Elise said.

I thought about the pile of them on the motel bedspread, right after I'd seen the pregnancy test, and spit them into my hand. One pink line and you're okay. Two pink lines and your life is over. My sister was pregnant. I'd forget and then I'd remember and be shocked all over again. Not only had she had sex, but she had gotten pregnant. Months from now, we could be sitting here with a baby between us, its little baby hands and baby feet, its baby mouth trying to latch itself onto our breasts.

Our parents didn't know, of course. Our parents were oblivious, Elise said, and quite possibly stupid, but I didn't agree. I thought our mother might be psychic.

Elise picked up the bag of snacks and flung it at me. I tied it in a knot and closed my eyes. I hadn't been sleeping well again. I wasn't a good sleeper, my mother had said once, and I liked the way it sounded—as if sleeping was a talent, or a skill I had yet to learn. I'd wake up in the middle of the night from a bad dream or because I had to pee and lay there for hours thinking about things that didn't bother me at all during the day. Other times, I forgot I was a bad sleeper, but I hadn't forgotten since we'd left Montgomery. The secret to a lot of things was to forget, but I was always remembering.

"Welcome to Texas," our mother said.

"The great state of Texas," said our father.

Elise showed me a picture of an RV on her phone. It said HAVE YOU HEARD THE AWESOME NEWS? THE END OF THE WORLD IS ALMOST HERE! "Listen to this," she said. "'Greta Burrows, an obese, middle-aged woman who spent the morning leaning out the window shouting on a bullhorn, picked up some Visine and a box of Kleenex at the local Rite Aid.' I bet she also picked up some Cheetos. And probably some MUNCHIES, too."

"Which leg of the tour is that?" I asked.

"Florida. Greta's the one that left the door to her house open—not unlocked, but *wide open*. And she won't say how many kids she has or if she has a husband because the only thing that matters is warning people."

"That's hardcore."

"I know, right?"

"I should get y'all a bullhorn," our father said.

"I'd use a bullhorn," Elise said. She tried to roll down her window, but it was on child-lock, so she cupped her hands around her mouth and shouted into the front seat: "Repent or die! The sun'll turn red and drip blood! Your neighbors will perish in grizzly accidents!"

"Elise!" our mother said.

"They won't be accidents," our father said, "oh no, they won't be accidents at all."

————

Our father pulled off into a combination Pilot/McDonald's truck plaza. He put the car in park and sorted through the maps on the side of his door. In a field next to the gas station, an oil derrick pumped lazily.

"What are we doing?" I asked.

"Change of plans—I know there's one in here somewhere. Here we go." He handed the map to our mother and put his elbow on the back of his seat, turned around to look at us. "I need to apologize," he said. "I've been doing y'all a disservice. You can't experience this great land of ours from the interstate. It's all Taco Bells and Targets."

Elise and I looked at each other. We didn't feel we were being done any disservice. We liked Taco Bell and Target.

"From here on out, we'll be taking the highway and eating at places called Restaurant," he said. "I want you to experience the real America before it's too late, the places where real people live and worship." He didn't care if it was going to cost us time. Time would soon be made irrelevant.

"Okay," Elise said, "but I'm not staying in any fleabag motels with a bunch of drug addicts. I want to stay at Holiday Inns."

"We haven't stayed at a Holiday Inn *yet*," I said.

"We won't be staying with drug addicts," our mother said, taking the clip-on part of her sunglasses off. Cleaning her glasses was a nervous habit, like our father pausing to survey his surroundings, like my fake yawning.

"And I'm not going to any roadside zoos, either," Elise said, looking at me because I'd wanted to see some Cajuns feeding alligators in Louisiana.

"What if there's snakes?" I said. "You'd want to see snakes."

"No, I wouldn't. Why would I want to see snakes?"

"You used to have a snake."

"It was a tiny little garden snake," she said, "and I was like seven."

"We aren't going to any zoos," our father said. "We don't have the money for that kind of stuff."

"I bet we could save some people," I said.

"That's the idea," he said. "That's the spirit!" I thought of our cousin, a blonde on his side with a haircut our mother had called a Mary Lou Retton. When I was eleven, I'd gone with him to pay for a motel room for this cousin. He'd been out of work again and we'd scraped together the money in loose change and small bills.

This woman was dead now. She had been beaten to death in a different motel room, in a different city. I remembered the name of it because it was odd—the Admiral Benbow in Jackson, Mississippi. I had no memory of her except from pictures and family reunion slide shows, though my mother said she'd babysat us when we were little, when she was just a high school girl.

Our father got out and slipped three quarters into the air machine.

Elise opened her door. "Oh my God," she said. "It must be a hundred and ten out here."

"Hundred and four inside the car," our mother said. "And don't let your father hear you say that."

"It's a figure of speech," she said.

"*You* don't mind if we say 'oh my God?'" I asked, and my mother said of course she minded, it was sacrilegious. Then she took out her phone and called one of her sisters, but I couldn't tell which one—their voices all sounded alike: loud and slow with accents we had somehow escaped. She had three sisters and one brother and they were always calling each other, even though, except for my uncle in west Alabama, they lived within a few miles of each other in Montgomery. They liked to talk about who died and who had cancer and who was getting a divorce. They liked to be the first to know so they could call each other up and relay the bad news. But whoever was on the other end got another call and had to go.

Our father often questioned her loyalty—asked whether she was with us or with them. Since he wasn't close to his own family, his loyalty was unquestionably to us. We weren't sure if he disliked our mother's family because they were Catholic or if he just couldn't stand for her affections to be split.

I found a spot of something on my t-shirt, guacamole maybe, that scratched off in flakes. The black King Jesus Returns! t-shirts did a good job of hiding sweat stains and mustard, and it made me appreciate this required uniform. Our mother was wearing one, too, a large that hung loose and shapeless over her hips. Our father had on one of his no-iron Brooks Brothers shirts; today's was green-and-white striped. His sister gave him gift cards at Christmas. She got them for putting a lot of stuff on her credit card.

"Will we still get to eat at McDonald's?" I asked.

"Your father won't give up McDonald's," our mother assured us.

"I like McDonald's in the morning."

"We know you do, Jess," Elise said, "we know." She fanned herself with a magazine. It had the swim-suited bodies of celebrities on the cover, their eyes blacked out with rectangular boxes. My parents didn't like Elise's music or clothes or the TV shows she watched or the magazines she read. They didn't like most of her friends or any of her boyfriends. They used to have long discussions with her about God's intentions for her life, and our father would tell her she was going to hell and she'd be there all alone—she'd be in hell *all alone*—but now they pretty much let her do what she wanted as long as she maintained appearances. As long as we were all in church every Wednesday and Sunday, sitting quietly in our nice clothes.

The main difference between Elise and me was that I was a liar. I did things our parents disapproved of, but I did them quietly. I didn't even have to be all that quiet about it because she made so much noise it was easy for them to overlook me altogether. I'd seen every episode of *Jersey Shore* and *16 and Pregnant*. I read Elise's magazines when she was finished, and I'd once sucked the gas from a can of whipped cream and gotten high for about thirty seconds.

"I'll be right back," Elise said, getting out.

I opened my door and ran to catch up with her. A boy watched us from the tinted window of a pickup, a cowboy hat in the middle of the dash and two dogs scrabbling over each other to bark at us from the bed.

The doors slid open and the cold air enveloped us.

We walked straight back to the bathroom and I stopped at the weight machine, tall and blinking. I hadn't weighed myself since we'd left home and I'd been eating everything in sight. I decided I didn't want to know and went into a stall. It had four locks, three of them broken. I pulled the top bar across and hovered while staring at a woman's feet in the stall next to mine. They were wide and sunburnt and her toenails were too small for her toes. They were the ugliest feet I'd ever seen, but she was wearing expensive-looking sandals and the nails were painted and I thought it was nice that she did what she could with them.

I opened the door to a girl standing in front of the mirror, singing along to "Family Tradition," which was being pumped throughout the building. I washed my hands while she took sections of her hair and sprayed it into different shapes with a giant can of aerosol hairspray. She was wearing tight black jeans tucked into a pair of leather boots, her face a smear of pinks and purples. She was probably a prostitute and would soon be caught up in a fireball, but now she was going about her business, making her hair as big as possible. I fixed my own hair in the mirror, running my fingers through it and then patting it down. I spent a lot of time looking at myself, trying to figure out what was wrong with my face.

I took my cell phone out of my purse and held it at different angles, but I couldn't figure out any way to take a picture without her noticing. I read a text from my mother I'd already read—"*American Idol* is starting!"—and deleted it.

Elise came out of a stall and the girl froze, can of hairspray suspended in the air. My sister smiled at her, an open friendly smile that said she was no threat at all.

"How much money do you have?" she asked.

"I don't know," I said, glancing at the girl. "Fifty?"

"You have more than that."

"You shouldn't have given all your money to that woman."

"Give me five."

I gave her a ten and opened the door with my elbow. Money had become precious now that I was earning it myself. I was bad at my job, making snow cones at a candy store, and no matter how much I got paid, it didn't seem like enough.

I walked back and forth in front of the drink cases a few times before selecting a Yoo-hoo. Then I stood in the candy aisle, trying to decide. The guy at the register was watching and I turned my back to him so it might look like I was preparing to slip something into my purse or down my shorts. I'd never stolen anything, but when people watched me so closely, it made me feel guilty, made me want to be caught and found innocent.

I chose a pack of Skittles and a King-Size Snickers, carefully considered a bag of caramel Bugles. Ever since our father had been diagnosed with diabetes, our mother had been trying to make us eat healthier—she'd stir-fry vegetables in PAM and bake chicken in corn flakes. She'd swapped the regular mayonnaise and cream cheese for low-fat versions that we immediately recognized and called her out on. And then she'd tried a different tactic. She began to make strange, foreign dishes we had no names for; the most recent had been a burnt-orange soup made with tomatoes, eggplants, and chickpeas.

"How much are these?" I asked the guy, picking a hard boiled egg out of a basket.

"Thirty-five cents," he said. He was freakishly tall with stick arms crossed in front of his chest.

"Thirty-five cents," I repeated.

He pushed his hair back from his face, and I placed the egg on the counter, stopped it from rolling. I paid for everything and loaded it into my purse, and he gave me sixteen cents back, which I dropped into the tray of leave-one-take-one pennies, which was maybe too much to leave in the tray of pennies.

Outside, the girl stood smoking a cigarette, a dog at her feet. In the sunlight, she wasn't pretty at all. She had a puffy scar beneath one eye, blackheads on the sides of her nose.

"Is that your dog?" I asked.

"No."

"What's his name?"

"I said it's not mine."

"What kind is it?"

"Are you deaf?" she asked. And then, "Blue heeler."

"Does he bite?"

"I dunno, I just found him here." I crouched down to pet him, and she said, "I've known heelers to bite, not the best people dogs. This one's okay, though, you can look at his eyes and tell." She started to say something else and stopped, as if remembering she had no reason to talk to me. I petted the dog's head, which was too small for its body, and thought about giving the girl some money to feed him, but I didn't want her to buy condoms or cigarettes with it.

I tried to think of other questions for my information-gathering mission, but everything I could think to ask could be answered in one or two words: *yes, no, fuck off.*

The dog looked at me and I looked at him and I had the feeling I got sometimes with dogs and babies, like they could see that I was bad, like they were waiting for me to lift my hand into the air and bring it down hard.

Elise came out eating a red, white, and blue popsicle—a rocket pop—the kind we used to buy from the ice-cream man in our neighborhood. "What's his name?" she asked.

The girl repeated what she'd told me, that she'd just found the dog, or the dog had found her. "I'm traveling," she added. "I can't have a dog with me all the time."

My sister held the popsicle out so it wouldn't drip on her shirt, leaned over to take another bite. "Where you headed?"

"Las Vegas," the girl said.

"Why Las Vegas?"

"Have you ever *been* to Las Vegas?"

"No."

"Then I can't explain it to you," she said.

The popsicle streamed down Elise's fist, trails of red and blue staining her hand.

"I'm going to stay at Paris," the girl said. "At night, the stars are all over the place like a real night sky. There's two bathrooms and a minibar with chocolate and cute little bottles of wine and you can look out and see the whole city."

She'd probably seen the hotel on the Travel Channel, that boring show with that boring Samantha Brown woman. I had no idea why anyone would have ever put that woman on television, let alone given her her own show.

———

In the car, my mother was listening to Joyce Meyer. "Repeat after me," Joyce said. "I don't have to bleed any more. I don't have to bleed." I liked the sound of it—not only the way she phrased it, but the idea that suffering was something I inflicted upon myself and I didn't have to do it any longer. All of my suffering could stop this very minute.

My mother and I liked Joyce Meyer, but my father would make her turn it off when he got in the car. He said she didn't consult the Bible, but I thought he disliked her because she was loud and opinionated, and worst of all, unattractive. I especially liked to watch her on TV, her matching pantsuits and careful makeup and the way she said amen over and over like it was a question. *Amen? Amen?* She couldn't stand it when the audience was quiet. She'd talk about her husband then, tell us something Dave said, and the men would be reminded she was just a wife and the women would be reminded that we were always only wives. But still, she was the one on stage while Dave sat in the audience waiting to be talked about.

I bet she had a lot of money and hardly ever gave any of it away. I bet she ate steak every night and slept in hotel rooms with thick, white carpet.

"Where's Dad?" I asked, taking a slug off my Yoo-hoo.

"The Waffle House didn't sit well with his stomach," she said.

"I guess we can add that to the list of places we can't eat anymore."

Elise got in the car and asked where Dad was.

"The bathroom," my mother said, checking her watch even though there was a clock in the middle of the dash.

"You're running a minute behind on every conversation," I said. "It's super annoying."

She leaned over and opened her hand: a pink lighter with the words "True Love" in red rhinestones. "Texans love to bedazzle some shit," she said. "I couldn't decide between this and one with Elvis's head on it—young Elvis. Have you ever seen pictures of young Elvis?"

"Of course."

"He was amazing," she said. "I see we're picking up Joyce Meyer. How wonderful."

"Joyce is preaching on obeying God and being blessed," I said.

"Isn't she always?"

"Unless she's trying to explain why bad things happen to good people."

"That's a tougher sell. What town are we in?"

"Beaumont," our mother said.

"Beaumont! I think that's where *Footloose* was set," Elise said. We loved Kevin Bacon, too. Kevin Bacon was his most beautiful in *Footloose*, primarily for the angry dance scene in the abandoned warehouse, even though you could tell it wasn't always actually Kevin Bacon. When the camera panned out, something was off—the torso too wide or the legs too long, something hard to put your finger on.

Our mother ejected the disc and placed it carefully back in its box. Elise and I watched our father stop to look around with his pleasant expression, his hands on his hips. He had biggish hips, almost womanly, that he was always calling attention to.

He got into the car making noises like he wanted someone to ask how his stomach was so he could tell us it wasn't good. He tried to stick the rearview mirror back into place again, and this went on until Elise burst out laughing and then I started laughing. I was afraid he'd get mad, but he just sighed and opened his Coke. He called it Cocola, which made me think of him as a little kid. Once he was just a little kid hunting and fishing to put food on the table after his father moved to Florida with a red-haired woman.

He took another swig and another, throwing his head back jerkily as he made his way to the bottom of the can. Then he handed it to our mother and put the car into DRIVE.

As we were about to pull out of the station, a yellow convertible plowed directly into a white car, slamming it head-on. The man in the white car flew through the windshield and landed in the road as the cars spun off in opposite directions. It was very loud and then it was quiet.

"Oh my God," Elise said.

My mother made the sign of the cross and my father backed up and parked in the spot we'd just pulled out of. We all got out. Both of the cars' radios were playing, tuned to the same station. The people in the convertible were still in there, but the man in the white car must not have been wearing his seatbelt. He was faceup in the street and there was blood everywhere. I knew he was dead.

I looked over at a couple of teenage girls next to a gas pump, their hands covering their mouths. And then one of them removed her hands and screamed. After that, everybody started moving. Elise dialed 911. My father jogged over to the convertible and another man ran to join him. My mother sent me inside to tell the freakishly tall guy, but he already knew, so I went back out and stood next to my mother and Elise, the Las Vegas girl, and her dog. We had just seen a man die. A man who had been alive only moments before, thinking about nothing or nearly nothing—wondering whether it was too early to have a drink, or if he might go for a swim this evening—things that were so inconsequential they were an insult to his life. He hadn't had a moment to prepare, would take all of his secrets with him.

I made up a hundred different scenarios. He was newly married to the woman of his dreams. He was a drug dealer, a felon, a preacher, a man with more children than he could afford to feed. He was depressed and thought about dying all the time. No matter who he'd been, though, he would be described in heroic terms, like everyone who died as a result of someone else's negligence. Perhaps he'd been going to the store for nothing more important than ice cream, an unnecessary trip he'd taken to get out of the house. I was sorry I'd never know him. If I knew even a little something, I might piece together a story for his life.

My father dragged a girl out of the passenger seat of the convertible, cradled her in his arms. She was nine or ten years old, tall and thin. My mother took my hand and began to pray, but I pulled away and left her there with Elise, ignoring their calls to come back.

The girl was Asian—Japanese—with long shiny hair in perfect order. She looked like she was asleep. When I was little we'd had a dog that had been hit by a car; my mother placed him in his bed, curled up, like he was napping. He'd looked perfect, not a spot of blood on him, and I couldn't believe he was dead. I'd sat with him for hours, waiting for him to open his eyes.

"Is she dead?" I asked.

"No," he said.

"How do you know?"

"She's breathing."

"Why doesn't she open her eyes?"

"I don't know," he said.

"Do you think she's in a coma?"

"I don't know," he said again.

I wanted him to know something. "It looks like she's asleep," I said. Wake up, I thought. *Wake up.*

The other man had pulled a woman out of the driver's side of the convertible. She was young and white and I wondered if she was the babysitter. The woman was alive, moaning softly, and then she sat up and screamed the most horrible scream I'd ever heard. And then she was shaking violently and screaming and the whole thing seemed like a bad television reenactment. No one was with the dead man. I walked over to him and crouched down, his face covered in blood and gashes. Elise and the Las Vegas girl joined me, watched as I touched his neck, which I wouldn't have had the nerve to do without them there.

"Don't do that," Elise said. "What're you doing?"

"Checking for a pulse."

"Do you feel anything?" the Las Vegas girl asked.

I moved my fingers around, searching for the artery.

An ambulance arrived and a medic hustled us out of the way, and then there were police cars and fire trucks and we were moved farther and farther out of the way until we were no longer a part of it. We stood with the others, watching as they loaded them onto gurneys, as they covered the man in the white car with a sheet. My mother and Elise were crying. The Las Vegas girl touched my sister's arm and they embraced. This seemed very strange and I tried to catch Elise's eye, but she wouldn't look at me.

I listened as those around us tried to work out what had happened, explaining it to the new people who'd arrived on the scene. They were already getting it wrong. We had seen it up close—we'd had the best view and I felt like they should be asking us. The convertible hadn't been turning into the gas station. They'd both been driving straight past each other when the convertible swerved into the path of the man in the white car, who was now dead. Who, I had decided, had been on an unnecessary errand to buy an unnecessary item. Maybe he hadn't even wanted the item, but had offered to get it for his girlfriend, a woman he hadn't loved enough to marry.

We stood there for another ten minutes, waiting for someone to involve us again, to ask us questions, but no one did. We got back in our car. Elise was still crying. I cried so infrequently that other peoples' tears surprised me, though they didn't surprise me now; my lack of tears surprised me. Why didn't I feel things the way others felt them? It wasn't that I didn't care about people. It was more like I couldn't really believe they were real. I dug my fingernails into my palm, hard.

I'd read somewhere that not caring about people was a sign of mental illness, but I didn't feel mentally ill.

"I have blood on me," my father said, holding up his hands and turning them slowly. It reminded me of that scene in *Back to the Future* where Michael J. Fox was disappearing because his parents hadn't kissed so he wasn't going to be born. He got out of the car and went inside. I looked at my own hands—they looked clean even though I had touched a bloody dead man. I had a dead man on me.

———

My father drove ten minutes in the wrong direction and no one said anything. I thought about the girl, whether she might be Chinese or Korean instead of Japanese. Why had I thought she was Japanese? I didn't know anyone who was Japanese.

Finally, Elise pointed out a butcher shop we'd passed earlier.

"Where's that map?" he asked.

My mother opened it, unfolding and unfolding until it filled the front seat. I looked at the back of her head, her thin hair fluffed up. I had her hair—fine and eager to fall out; we had to bend over and brush it upside down to make it look normal.

"We need to get on 90," my mother said, while my father kept driving the way we'd come.

"Tell me where to turn," he said.

"I think it's this way."

"Just tell me where to turn."

"The GPS is in the console," Elise said, but our father didn't like being told what to do by a machine. He'd turn too early or too late and there was no one to blame it on.

"There," our mother said, "now."

He jerked the wheel and took the exit left.

"Are there any wet wipes up there?" I asked.

My mother tossed me a package that had been opened long ago. They were dry but I rubbed them on my hands, anyway.

"Let me see that map," Elise said. Our mother passed it back and Elise spread it out, West Texas on my lap and East Texas on hers.

"I'm sad," I said. I didn't feel sad, but I thought saying it might help me feel it.

My mother turned and gave me a slight shake of her head.

"What?" I said. She didn't say anything. "What?" I said again. I sighed and tracked the highway with my finger.

"'Welcome to the great state of Texas,'" Elise read. "'Whether you are a visitor or a resident, I hope you take advantage of the vast and varied travel opportunities Texas offers.' Well, thank you. We certainly don't plan on it." She started Googling various towns along our route to see if there was anything worth seeing, though we knew we weren't going to stop. We didn't really want to stop. We only wanted to know what we were going to miss.

"We'll come really close to Mexico," I said. "Maybe we could cross the border."

"There are drug wars going on," our father said. He'd read a news story about a tourist town where the kids hadn't been in school since February because the drug cartels were demanding half the teachers' salaries so the teachers were refusing to teach. In response, the cartels were decapitating them and leaving their heads in the streets. I watched my mother to see if she'd put a hand on his arm or give him a look, but she didn't.

Elise flipped the map over and we studied the picture of the governor and his wife. They were handsome in the usual way of politicians: stiff-haired with closed-mouth smiles. The wife was blond, with pale skin and glassy eyes; she looked like a doll. The governor looked a little more reasonable, but not by much. Elise folded the map the wrong way and unfolded and refolded until she got it right.

I took the egg out of my purse, still intact.

"Where'd you get that?" Elise asked.

"The gas station."

"That's really gross."

"You think everything's gross."

"What is it? Did you get me one?" my father asked.

"It's an egg. And no, I didn't know you wanted one." I offered it to him and he agreed without hesitation, so I passed it up and opened my Snickers. I tore off a hunk and held it out to Elise, who shook her head. I was never going to be skinny like her. She said all I had to do was starve for a month, six weeks tops, but I couldn't do it. It might as well have been forever.

"Do you want some salt?" our mother asked, opening the glove box to search for a stray packet, but the egg was already gone. Elise was the only skinny one, and I was glad for it because I didn't want our whole family to be overweight—it would seem like a fundamental flaw, like something we'd never overcome.

Our father zigzagged through a small town in order to stay on the right highway, but then it split, one marked business and the other marked truck. After taking the business highway into a bricked and empty downtown, we learned to follow the one for trucks.

The next town we came to was nicer. There were a lot of stores—not just tire stores and gas stations, but shops selling pottery and cupcakes and seafood. The Texas flag hung in front of each one. Our mother looked back and forth, reading the signs aloud: HUCKLEBERRY'S SEAFOOD, LIGHTFOOT FLOORING, THE PLAY PEN, GOLDEN GIRLZ SALON, HOME BAKED.

"Angel Funeral Home," she continued. "The Jalapeno Tree. Save America Vote Republican. Lupe's Cantina."

"I bet Mexicans don't eat at The Jalapeno Tree," I said.

"I bet they don't eat at Lupe's Cantina, either," Elise said.

"I bet Lupe doesn't even *exist*," I said.

"The Palace Donuts didn't make it," our mother said, making the sorry clucking sound I hated. The sorry clucking sound that said she was happy the Palace Donuts hadn't made it. I couldn't figure her out. She seemed like a nice person, doing all of the nice things nice people did—visiting the sick and volunteering at church, sending flowers and thank-you notes, but when one of her best friends died, she hadn't even seemed sad about it. I kept asking about the woman, even though I hadn't liked her, a busybody who was always trying to draw junior high gossip out of me.

"Oh man, look at that," my father said, slowing to a crawl for an old man pushing a lawnmower across the highway. The man stopped in the middle of the road to give us a dirty look before continuing. Our father got a kick out of that and Elise took a picture of him with her phone. Then she started taking pictures of other things: the backs of our parents' heads, VFW posts, signs that read HISTORICAL MARKER 1 MILE, without ever indicating what it was they were marking.

At a stoplight, we pulled up behind a big shiny truck and my mother pointed out the bumper sticker—the state of Texas with a pistol across it: WE DON'T DIAL 911.

"Texas is scary," Elise said.

"It's all trucks and guns and meat," I said.

"And football," our father said. "They love football."

"We've seen *Friday Night Lights*," I said.

"That sounds familiar," Elise said, holding her phone in my

face. I pushed her hand away and she took a picture of my legs. "I hate all those things."

"You're a cheerleader," I said.

"It doesn't mean I like football."

"No, but you support football."

"I support hot guys in tight pants banging into each other," she said.

"Elise," our mother said, "please." She asked our father to do something about her, but he got distracted by a deer on the side of the road.

"Do you see it?" he asked. I knew he was talking to me, that I was the one he wanted to show it to.

"I don't see it," I said. I never saw anything on the side of the road unless it was dead.

"Right there, at the tree line. You can't miss it."

"I don't see it."

"It's *right there,*" he said. And then, "You missed it."

I hated the disappointment in his voice. "I never see anything," I said, remembering that the animals weren't going to be raptured. Our father had been trying to prepare us for a heaven without Cole, the dog we'd had for nine years. We'd dropped him off at the vet before leaving Montgomery. He hated being boarded so much and was shaking so bad I'd had to help my father get him inside.

Cole had had a stroke on New Year's Day and I'd taught him to walk again, fashioning a harness out of an old dress. I'd slept with him on the kitchen floor at night when he'd been unable to control his bladder, while the rest of them slept comfortably in their beds. It was the best thing I'd ever done and I reminded them of it constantly. Cole was fine now, though he ran crooked and couldn't catch squirrels anymore. I couldn't imagine any-place without him, without the small animals he loved to chase. That was my problem—I had no imagination—I couldn't imag-ine anything other than what I knew. The way time functioned, for example. Minutes. Waiting. How long a day could be. My biggest fear was that things would go on forever and there would never be any end. The idea of forever terrified me, even if we were in heaven and everything was great there. Surely, it would have to come to an end at some point. There would have to be something else. When I wanted to scare myself, I'd lay in bed and think *forever and ever and ever and ever and ever* until I thought I might go crazy.

Our father said heaven was going to be perfect in a way we couldn't even begin to comprehend because we'd never known anything like it. We'd be young and healthy and surrounded by our loved ones. There would be no fear and no hate and no war, happiness and pleasure like we'd never known. I was already young and healthy and surrounded by my loved ones and it didn't seem so great. And I wondered how good happiness and pleasure could be without their opposites to compare them to. If everyone was beautiful, what would beauty even mean? What would I have to strive for?

"What's the caravan up to?" I asked.

"Eating at every food court in every mall in central Florida," Elise said, looking at her phone. "Greta's a big Sbarro fan."

"After they eat at Sbarro, I bet they cruise up and down the main drag and stop at Sonic for cherry limeades."

"Swap the limeades for Oreo Blasts and you'd be right," she said. Then she started laughing.

"What?" I asked.

"Nothing."

"What's so funny?"

"I just remembered something," she said.

"What?"

"Nothing," she said, angrily. I hated when she wouldn't tell me what she was laughing about; it was like she did it to remind me that my life wasn't as amusing as hers.

We passed fields of cows, tails swinging, standing in the sun. They had their heads down, eating grass. Just eating grass all day long. I fingered my gold-plated ring on my gold-plated chain. The ring said PURITY on the outside; on the inside it had my initials: JEM. It was cheap and ugly and Elise had the same one hanging from her own chain. We'd gone to a purity ball, made pledges. We'd worn white dresses, and our father had gotten down on one knee in a school gymnasium to slip the rings on our fingers: first Elise, then me. This had been four years ago, before I'd even gotten my period. Before we'd known better, Elise said, but we'd worn them so long they were a part of us. I felt naked when I took it off.

My memories of that night were good ones. There had been wedding cake and steak and a hot dip made with crabmeat. I befriended a young black girl, a pretty girl with gray eyes. I had never known a black girl before. The school we went to was all-white. The neighborhood we lived in was all-white. I only saw black people at the mall, or driving around in their cars.

———

Our father scanned radio stations and stopped at a program called *Revive Our Hearts*, the woman talking about Noah and the end times. The end times seemed to be all that was left to talk about. The woman said if you read the Old Testament, you would see that it had been necessary for God to wipe out the world in a catastrophic flood and it was necessary for Him to wipe it out again.

"The Flood couldn't have been worldwide—there isn't enough water in the oceans," Elise said. "It would have taken five times the water in the oceans."

Our father wasn't taking the bait. He turned the radio off and pumped the gas, the car lurching and coasting, lurching and coasting. He did this when he was agitated or wanted to annoy us. If we said something, it would go on longer, but I usually said something anyway to point out what an asshole he was. This time I kept my mouth shut. It was probably making Elise nauseous.

I counted down the miles to the next town—22, 15, 9, 6, 4, 2—and then we were cruising into a little nothing town.

In front of a boarded-up convenience store, a fat woman manned a table full of colorful junk. We passed a man selling puppies out of a cardboard box, a young girl holding one up to get a look at its eyes. We passed a Subway, a tiny post office, and a tinier library. I thought about all these people living in all these towns and how I'd never know them, and something about it seemed sad and strange—maybe it was just that I'd never thought of them before, that they had never occurred to me at all.

"I feel sick," Elise said. "Can I sit up front?"

"Can we change at the next stop?" our father said.

"No, I need to sit up front *now*."

He pulled into a McDonald's and Elise and our mother swapped. Then we decided we might as well get ice cream.

We were all in a better mood after that.

"Hi," I said, looking over at my mother, a chocolate shake wedged between my thighs. She looked at me and smiled, her eyes blinking behind the blue lenses. She took my hand and I let her hold it a minute before pulling away.

I picked up my milkshake and turned to the window. At some point, my feelings for my parents had changed. I mostly felt nothing and couldn't think of anything to say to them, but it was periodically broken by a brief, crushing feeling, a love so intense that there was nothing to do but reject it altogether.

————

We stopped for an early supper at a barbeque restaurant/gas station. Most of the gas stations were attached to something now. In Louisiana, we'd stopped at one attached to a tanning salon and Elise had tanned, cooking the baby while the rest of us ate shrimp po boys.

A handsome soldier held the door, called Elise and me "ma'am."

"Thank you, sir," Elise said, nodding at him.

"Thanks," I said, so he would look at me and see that I was separate. He touched my shoulder for the briefest of seconds. *I love you*, I thought, and it felt like the truth.

The place was full of army men in their army hats and pants, stiff long-sleeved shirts. The material looked thick and uncomfortable, but they somehow managed to look fresh. We ordered at the front, but there wasn't a four-top available, so my parents sat at one two-top and we sat at another, far enough away that we could pretend we were alone. I watched Elise pull the ponytail holder from her hair and comb it out with her fingers. She moved her head from side to side to gather all the stray pieces before putting it up again. The process took a long time, a minute at least. I wanted to talk about the Japanese girl and the dead man, but Elise would accuse me of dwelling on the negative. Debbie Downer, she liked to call me.

Her phone dinged. She read the message and smiled as she typed her response. As soon as she set it down, it dinged again. I searched the room and located the handsome soldier. He was by far the best-looking soldier in the room, tall and tan and broad-shouldered. He could pick me up, no problem.

"Dan's so cute," she said, showing me the picture he'd sent her. He was giving the camera an exaggerated sad face—bottom lip turned out, head tilted—so he must have done something wrong. "Don't you think he's cute?"

"I guess. His eyes are kind of bloodshot." I thought of the two of them watching TV together on the couch, how they created a space in which no one was welcome. I didn't like Dan. He was always turning words around, calling Facebook "the book of faces" and stuff like that. Elise looked out the window and I stared at the delicate veins on her temple, blue and winding like rivers on a map. They were the only thing about her that wasn't pretty.

Our father brought our food on plastic plates with little dividers. "Which is which?"

"Mine's the one without pork," Elise said.

He set them down, giving her the pork plate, and bowed his head.

"We can pray by ourselves, Dad," she said. She glanced up at him and went back to her phone. He probably hated having daughters—we didn't fish or hunt and we were having sex with boys, or would eventually have sex with them. I kicked her under the table and my father put his hand on my back. It went up and down a few times and he walked back to his table.

"You're a jerk," I said. I swapped our plates and picked up a greasy bottle of barbeque sauce, squeezed some onto a clean spot. "I'm going to throw your phone across the room."

"Just leave me alone for a minute," she said. "I haven't talked to Dan in days."

"More like twelve hours." I bowed my head and then looked to see if she was following my lead; she wasn't. I took a bite of potato salad. The tallest, most handsome army man would not be swayed by Elise's beauty. He would brush my hair and be careful untangling the knots. He'd hoist me onto his shoulders at parades so I could catch all the beads.

I got out my phone and looked at it—no one ever texted me.

I thought about texting Shannon, but there was nothing to say, so I turned the sound off so I wouldn't have to hear it not ringing and beeping. Shannon was my best friend, though she complained constantly and blamed others for everything. She'd tell me about all of the things she did for people and how they took advantage, insisting I wasn't one of these takers, that I was one of the few exceptions, but this conversation typically occurred after I'd borrowed her clothes or spent the night at her house two weekends in a row. I took another bite of potato salad and shook some salt onto the pile. I took another bite and another until it was gone and moved onto the baked beans. When the beans were done, I started in on my sandwich. I was starving and knew it wasn't food I wanted, but it had somehow become my focus.

"I wonder if these beans were cooked with bacon," Elise said, and her phone dinged again.

"The other day I was eating egg-drop soup and there were all these tiny little bits of ham in it," I said. "You're probably eating meat all the time and don't even know it. Seaweed salad, too— there's fish in it. 'Contains fish,' it says on the package, when you buy it at the grocery store."

She ignored me and continued typing.

"Your texting and Googling are distracting me from the purpose of this trip," I said. "I don't even know how you live in the world." I had heard someone say this once—*I don't even know how you live in the world*. I liked the way it sounded. I took another bite of my sandwich. A piece of pork fell in my lap, barely missing the napkin.

She set her phone down. "You know why we're really here, don't you?"

"No—why are we *really* here?"

"Because Dad lost his job again," she said.

"No," I said.

"Yes."

"What happened?"

"I don't know."

"Yes you do."

"No, really, I don't, or I'd tell you," she said.

"I thought it was going fine."

"We always think that," she said. "He always makes us think that."

We were quiet for a minute. "At least mom has a job," I said. "She'll never get fired."

"Sure, mom has a job."

Our mother taught third grade, had taught third grade when I was in third grade, the year my life had taken a bad turn. All of a sudden, you were either popular or unpopular, and boys liked you or they didn't, a decision they made as a group. Before this, there had just been the kids we'd all stayed away from: the masturbators and scissor thieves and glue eaters, anyone who brought a separate container of mayonnaise in their lunch bag.

She sighed and balled up her napkin on her plate. She was like girls on TV—all they did was spin the spaghetti round and round their forks. I looked at my legs pressed against the yellow plastic, pale and wide. I placed a hand on one thigh and imagined slicing the fat away, how thin I would want them if I could just cut it off. They wouldn't have to be as skinny as Elise's.

"We shouldn't judge him," I said.

"Why not?"

My army man stood to leave—smiling and shaking hands. He grabbed a stocky guy by the elbow as he shook, the other hand clapping the guy's back.

"He had a hard life," I said. "We didn't have to live his life."

"So what?" she said.

"So we should have some compassion."

"Stop," she said.

"*You* stop." I took my plate to the trashcan and then went to the bathroom, which was cowboy-themed, the toilet paper unspooling from a piece of twine. When I came out, a man was standing there. He asked me if the bathroom was clean and in proper working order and I said that it was, and this pleased him. After that I wandered around the store, weaving in and out of aisles considering things I didn't want—motor oil and coffee filters and saltines, packages of Imodium A-D and Motrin. My army man was gone forever. I'd never sit on his shoulders at a parade, high up, safe from everyone and everything.

———

Soon after we got back on the road, the sky turned green and the lightning began, splitting the sky in half. I hadn't seen lightning like that in a long time, maybe ever, though I'd once seen a tornado spinning off in the distance when my father and I went to pick up Elise from cheerleading practice. As soon as the funnel was gone, it was like something out of a dream.

The wind blew the car from side to side. It blew trash out of the beds of pickups, bags and boxes my father weaved around in case there was anything inside them. A few fat drops hit the windshield, and then there was the quiet moment while we waited for the downpour to begin.

The rain came all at once, battering the car. Our father slowed to a crawl and put on his hazards as eighteen-wheelers hurtled past. The windows fogged and he yelled at our mother to fix them so she fiddled with the temperature control: blasts of hot air followed by blasts of cold. I took off my seatbelt and scooted forward, my head between their shoulders—I couldn't make out anything except the brake lights of the car in front of us and the occasional glimpse of white line.

My father pulled onto the shoulder and put the car in park.

"We could get rear-ended here," my mother said, as the vehicles whooshing by rattled our doors.

"This shoulder's big," he said. It *was* a big shoulder, much bigger than the ones in Alabama. Cars passed on them, used them as extended turn lanes. There was a whole protocol to this big shoulder we hadn't figured out yet.

My mother shoved my head into the backseat like she did with Cole. "Put your seatbelt back on," she said.

I put it on and looked out the window. I liked to track the drops, but there was just a smear.

Elise stuck her feet in my lap and told me to rub.

"Why? Are they swollen?" I asked, fingering one of her

smooth, red toenails. She punched me in the arm so hard I'd probably have a bruise in the morning. I closed my eyes. When I saw the lightning flash through my eyelids, I counted the seconds until thunder.

After a while, the rain slacked and our father pulled back onto the road, but it was the same as before: nothing but brake lights and glimpses of white line.

"It's hard to believe Noah was the only man worth saving," Elise said.

"If He thought Noah was the only man worth saving, he was," our father said.

"I mean, how many people were alive back then? And they were *all* bad? That's just really hard to believe."

I pressed my forehead to the glass and banged it softly while Elise argued the scientific evidence against the Flood, which seemed like very solid evidence despite my unwillingness to listen, and then our father argued what was meant by "the world." He spoke of ancient wood and seven types of mussels and his evidence seemed solid as well. But then Elise got angry—she always got angry first—and he said, "Why don't we save it for this evening, when we aren't in the middle of a dee-luge?"

I'd never heard him use this word before and didn't think he had pronounced it correctly. "I don't want to save it for this evening," I said. "I want to watch *Honey, I Shrunk the Kids* and order pizza. Can we order pizza?"

Nobody said anything.

"Hello?" I said. It came out sounding horrible.

"If we can find someplace to deliver it," my mother said.

The road narrowed into one lane for roadwork and my father bumped an orange cone; it wobbled but didn't go down. My mother put a hand on the back of his neck and told him he was doing a good job, which she did when he was doing a bad job, and I got the spacy out-of-body feeling I got sometimes, like I wasn't real, like nothing was real so nothing mattered. We could drive off a cliff and I wouldn't care. And then the feeling was gone and I was back inside my body. I turned my hands palm-up and slowly moved my fingers, thinking, *These are your hands. You are moving your hands.* Sometimes I found this incredible, but now it just seemed dumb. Of course they were my hands. Of course I could move them.

By the time the rain stopped, our father's nerves were shot.

At the next town, he pulled into a motel in the kind of place he was trying to save us from—two motels, two fast-food restaurants, a gas station, and a bar—but all the small towns were like this. The factories had closed and people were left with a few places to regroup on their way to someplace better, except they didn't go anyplace better. How did they survive? I bet most of them were on disability or welfare.

We stayed in the car while he went into the office, the radio playing Taylor Swift and Garth Brooks. Halfway through Martina McBride, he gave the thumbs-up and we got out. The pavement wasn't wet. It looked like it hadn't rained here at all.

"Did we get our own room?" Elise asked.

"Not tonight," he said.

"I thought you were putting everything on your credit card."
The way Elise figured it, the credit card was free money since my
father didn't believe he'd be around to pay it back. She didn't
understand why we weren't staying at four-star hotels, sleeping
in plush, king-sized beds.

While we gathered our stuff, our mother pointed out that
the motel was being renovated: TVs had been wheeled outside;
bed frames and mattresses leaned against the walls; carpets
rolled and stacked. Our room, however, didn't look like it
had been renovated since the place had been built, a very long
time ago.

We set our luggage down and our father went to get ice, first
thing, like he always did. I went to the bathroom, which was
handicapped—bars everywhere and a sticky mat in the tub so
you wouldn't slip and bust your head, which made me not want
to take a shower after all. I propped an elbow on a bar and listened to Elise complain. Only drug addicts wore black t-shirts,
she said, and boys who ate foot-long sandwiches and read manga
in the lunchroom. Girls like Elise didn't even sit in the lunchroom—they sat in the little waterless ditch in the courtyard,
their legs stretched out so they could get a suntan. They passed
around bags of grapes and baby carrots because they found eating in public humiliating, and if they had to do it, they would
eat only foods that were clean and neat.

I opened the door and scooted past them, peeled the spread
off the bed closest to the bathroom. It was smooth and silky on
top but pilled underneath. I peeled back the top sheet and looked
for the short black hairs that were often woven into the thread. I

didn't see any so I got in and pulled the sheet up to my chin. It smelled clean, like bleach, and I thought of a show I'd seen about pests people couldn't get rid of. The family with bedbugs had closed them up in a suitcase and carried them home from a motel just like this one. The bugs were hardy and adapted to survive, moving up and down the stairs on the children's stuffed animals.

I listened to the sounds of renovation—things falling and being ripped out—while Elise and my mother droned on in the background. My mother spoke in the slow, controlled voice she'd been using a lot lately, a voice that begged us not to give her a hard time.

I got out of bed, opened the door, and stepped outside. The motel was two-story and horseshoe-shaped, the lot nearly full. I didn't see my father. A worker stepped out of the room next to ours; he was small and covered in a fine white dust.

"What are you doing?" I asked.

"Putting in carpet," he said.

I nodded and we shared a moment.

"Do you want new carpet in your room?" he asked.

I tried to think of something to say. Did he think we lived here? "Not today," I said, and he went back into the room he'd come out of. I closed the door and got back in bed. I wasn't gathering enough information. I tried to think of what else I could have asked him but couldn't come up with anything. I'd have had to start at the beginning. What was his name? Where was he born? Did he have a wife? Kids? But all of these things seemed meaningless.

"Fine," Elise said. "I'll wear King Jesus tomorrow if you wash it. I'll wear it for the rest of my life if you want."

"Jess, get me the detergent out of my carry-on," my mother said. "Come on, take 'em off."

We took off our shirts and threw them at her. Then we put on the Old Navy tank tops we liked to sleep in, fast, before our father returned. They were Christmas-themed—mine was red with white snowflakes and hers was white with red candy canes. For some reason, we only thought to buy them at Christmas.

"I wish you'd just let me stay home," Elise said. "We're working on a new routine and I'm going to be behind." She sat at my feet and fell between my legs. I kicked and scooted over and she came clambering up the bed and stuck her face in mine.

"We're not going back," I said, as dramatically as possible.

She put her finger up my nostril.

"Stop molesting me," I said, throwing the covers over my head.

I didn't want to go to heaven if Elise wasn't going to be there. I'd have to take my chances on earth. We'd make our way home and find Cole, or he'd find us, and then we'd locate the key to the gun case and catalogue the contents of the pantry before planting a garden in the wide, flat backyard, the place where we had always imagined a pool. She'd give birth to a healthy baby girl, or maybe a boy—our own boy. And I'd work hard all day and at night I'd be so tired it wouldn't occur to me to sleep badly. But then I thought about every postapocalyptic movie I'd ever seen and how we wouldn't be able to stay there because men would want our guns and our food. They'd want us to have their babies in order to repopulate the world, all of the pretense of love gone.

———

"Forget it," Elise said, sitting up abruptly. "I've changed my mind. I'm not wearing it again until Saturday, you can tell Dad that."

"Tell Dad what?" our father asked, opening the door. "You're wearing those shirts, they cost me twenty dollars."

"Each?" I said.

"That's right, each. There's only one ice maker working in this entire motel. This wouldn't happen at a Days Inn." He set the bucket on the table. He was partial to Days Inns. He had brand loyalty: Colgate, Maxwell House, Ivory soap.

"You're the one who stopped here," Elise said.

"I don't like Days Inns. I always find little nests of hair in the bathroom," I said. "It's like they don't even pretend to clean it."

"But the ice makers work," he said. He took off his glasses and held the bridge of his nose. Then he opened his eyes and looked blindly around the room. I hardly ever saw him without his glasses—he looked like someone who had been asleep for a long time and had just woken up.

Our mother squeezed the water out of our shirts while he chased a fly around the room with a newspaper. Then she went to the bathroom and did her business, silence punctuated by long airy farts, as our father continued to pursue the fly. Elise and I watched him with the blankest faces we could muster. When our mother came out, she washed her hands and made their drinks—a Sprite for herself and a whiskey for our father. She tried to hand the cup to him, but he was busy taking everything out of his suitcase: stacks of no-iron shirts, bundles of socks, a pile of tighty-whities.

In the doorway, they turned to us.

"We'll be at the pool," our mother said. Our father took a sip of his drink and made a face like it was too strong before closing the door.

"Finally," Elise said. "Good Lord." She rocked back and forth so the headboard knocked against the wall.

I searched for something to listen to on my iPod, scrolled through each of my playlists. Before leaving Montgomery, I'd made a *Heaven* mix and Elise had made an *End of the World* mix, but I was already tired of the songs I'd chosen. I decided on a mix labeled *Jogging*, though I never jogged. It hurt my knees.

Elise got out of bed and turned the air conditioner on high, checked the closet for extra pillows. She found one and launched it at my head.

"I can't believe they left the liquor. Is this some kind of test?"

"What?" I asked, taking out an earbud.

"Maker's Mark," she said, "whiskey." She took the bottle out of our mother's carry-on and held it up to the light like she might find something floating.

"Put it back."

"What?"

"You shouldn't drink," I said.

"I'll put some water in it and they'll never know."

"That's not why," I said. I'd found the First Response box in a trash can in Biloxi, faceup, like she'd wanted me to find it. That day, our father had stopped driving after a couple of hours and we'd spent the afternoon feeding the seagulls on the beach; they'd taken the chips right out of our hands. When I confronted her, she set the plastic stick on the table—the lines so brightly pink they glowed. Then she called Pizza Hut and paid for a half-veggie-half-sausage with her own money. I hadn't asked any questions, how far along she was or if she might want to keep it. We ate the entire pizza while watching *Willy Wonka & the Chocolate Factory*, the old one with Gene Wilder.

"Life occurs at conception," I said.

"Do you just repeat everything people tell you?"

"I've thought about it plenty. And it doesn't matter when the baby becomes a baby. If you let it grow long enough, it's a baby. This debate about when, *exactly*, it becomes a baby is stupid."

"I don't want to talk about it," she said.

"And you just repeat everything people tell you, too. Only it's the opposite thing I repeat." I thought I'd made a good point, which she confirmed by not saying anything. But maybe she wouldn't have to go through with it—she wouldn't have to have the baby or kill it—because we'd be saved. And after we were saved, the great storms and fires would descend upon the earth and then the earth would explode, and after it had exploded, it would be sucked up by a black hole followed by a quiet that was so quiet it would blow your eardrums out.

I wanted to believe we were special. I wanted to believe all of it—heaven and happiness and joy unlike anything I'd ever known.

"Okay," she said. "Life occurs at conception and we're going to heaven and it's going to be fucking awesome."

"You have to believe it."

"I wish you'd stop telling me what I have to believe. I've never been to church once—not once—and felt the presence of God, or anything else. So what exactly do you want me to believe in?" She handed me a cup and sat on our parents' bed.

"I don't want this," I said.

"So don't drink it. Answer me, what should I believe in?"

"It's about faith. You have to have faith," I said, realizing it was my own faith that was the issue. Elise had already decided God didn't exist and she was okay with it. I wanted to go back to the time when I hadn't thought about whether or not I believed, when I'd gone to church and Sunday school and passed out tracts and it never occurred to me to question any of it. Now everything was in question, all at once, and it mattered.

"What about you?" she said. "Do you feel the presence of God when you're in church, or do you just stare at peoples' asses and try not to yell curse words at the top of your lungs? Because that's what I do. Or I play hangman with you. I like those little sushi pencils."

I stuck my tongue in the cup—whiskey on ice, undrinkable. I didn't say anything, but she kept looking at me, waiting. "I count colors," I said. "How many people are wearing purple or yellow or green?"

"That's just sad."

"It's always some odd color that everybody's wearing, like half the congregation woke up and decided to wear orange."

"Wow," she said. "You're really boring. It must be really boring to be you."

"Sometimes I count fat people or bald heads."

"Bor-ing."

I spent most of my time, however, looking around at the other families, trying to determine how we stacked up. I looked at bodies and faces, hair and clothes and demeanors. We were usually pretty high up, because of Elise and my mother's church involvement.

"On Saturday night, I'm going to take off all my clothes and leave them on the grass at whatever shithole motel we're staying in, and then I'm going to hide in a bush and watch everybody freak out," she said.

"Good for you."

We sat there for a while, not saying anything. She drank her whiskey. I looked at my feet. I needed to do something with my feet.

"This isn't the first time this has happened, you know. Every generation's predicted the end of the world. We can't control war or unemployment or drug addiction or poverty but we can predict an end to these things, which makes them seem not so bad." She picked up her phone and typed while I waited, fingering the birthmark on my thigh. It was pale and Jamaica-shaped. As far as birthmarks went, it was nice.

"Okay," she said, "William Miller, a Baptist pastor, predicted the end of the world in March of 1844 but it didn't come so he revised it to April and then *that* didn't happen so he changed it to October. Jehovah's Witness founder Charles Russell said the end would come in 1874 and then 1914 and then 1918 and finally 1975, which would be so long after he was dead he wouldn't have to worry about changing it again. And then this guy, Marshall, has also predicted the end before. And when he's wrong a second time, he'll say he miscalculated and give us a new date—man's miscalculation, not God's, of course, never God's—and we'll be doing this all over again."

"Not me," I said.

She set her phone down. "Now let's pretend we're on vacation and having fun."

"I am having fun," I said. My bra strap slipped down my arm so I unhooked it and pulled it through my shirt. All of my bras were hand-me-downs from Elise, too small and worn out. "To the Pacific Ocean," I said, raising my whiskey. "May there be dolphins and no jellyfish."

We knocked our cups together, spilling some onto the floor, and brought them to our lips. I kept mine clamped tight. I'd had alcohol before but I'd never been drunk. At parties, I'd go behind a bush and pour my drink out, or shut myself in a bathroom and dump most of it down the sink. I'd once held my can sideways like I was so intoxicated I'd forgotten how to hold it until a boy asked me what the hell I was doing and I'd found it didn't work that way. I didn't know how it worked, but I had seen what people could do when they were drunk—Shannon cried and locked herself in bathrooms. She'd once given a stranger a blowjob in a parking lot.

I watched the liquid on top of the carpet, not seeping in.

"I miss Cole," Elise said, braiding a chunk of her hair. She could have been on TV she was so pretty. She was so pretty she had gone and gotten herself pregnant.

"I bet he's depressed without us," I said.

"Of course he's depressed—they keep him locked up in a cage with his own shit and only let him out once a day."

"That's terrible," I said.

"And I miss Dan."

It occurred to me Dan might not be the father, that it might be Abe, but she wasn't going to mention Abe because he'd broken up with her and started having sex with her best friend, Laura Lee, or maybe he'd been having sex with Laura Lee all along. The baby was Abe's—I knew this suddenly and clearly—and for a moment I was glad. But then I felt like an awful person. If God could see my heart, I'd never be saved, and of course he could see my heart. He was God.

"Maybe if I'm holding Cole in my arms he'll get to come with us," I said. "Like *Bill and Ted's Excellent Adventure.*"

She stacked her pillows and readjusted. "These pillows are too high. I knew we should have brought our own."

"But we'd forget them and the maids would give them to their grubby children."

"I'm going to get a crick in my neck," she said.

"That's a funny word."

She smiled at me and said, "I need to go to the store. Do you want anything?" But then she took the knife out of her pocket, opened it and started trimming the frayed pieces of blue jean from her shorts, making a little pile on the bedspread. She was the only girl I knew who carried a pocketknife. She'd found it while hiking. Our father said it was an excellent find—an expensive knife in good condition.

"Our movie's about to start," I said.

She held out her cup. "Hit me one more time and put some water in it."

I poured more than I should have and she drank it down. "I wish you'd stay," I said.

"I'll be right back." She took some money out of her wallet and folded it into her pocket. "If they come back, tell 'em I'm trying to score some weed," she said, and went out the door.

I checked to see how much she had—fifty-eight dollars, nearly as much as I had. I took two fives and dropped them into my purse, and then carried the bottle to the bathroom and held it under the faucet, filling it past the level it had been. I thought about the Japanese girl and how she'd looked asleep but was probably dead, her insides a jumble of smashed organs spilling blood all over the place. I put the bottle back in my mother's carry-on and looked around at the shirts dripping on the carpet, our clothes and shoes everywhere. Despite all our stuff, the room felt emptier than when we'd walked in.

I poured out my drink and rinsed the cups, put my toothbrush in one of them. Then I took my phone outside and sat against the door. The workers were gone, and other than a pair of goggles, there was no evidence they'd been there.

———

It was eight-ten and eight-twenty and eight-thirty and my parents would be back any minute. I was tired but knew I wouldn't sleep well because I was thinking about how tired I was and how much I needed to get a good night's sleep, which was exactly what you shouldn't do. You should go about your business like you're not even tired. You should stay out of bed as long as you can. I'd probably get four or five hours and wake up when it was still dark out, lie in bed waiting for the birds. Every morning the birds sounded different because they were different birds.

A man in a room across from me opened his door. He was black and muscled, tall and bald and handsome. He looked like a soap opera star.

He stood there for a moment with the light behind him, and then turned and said something to the woman in bed. She was plump and white with long dark hair, wearing only her panties. The woman gestured to the man to close the door, but he left it open, walked over to his car, and took something out of the trunk. Then he walked off in the same direction as Elise— toward the bar and gas station. The woman got out of bed with her breasts swinging and slammed the door.

A minute later, Elise came walking back across the parking lot with a paper bag in her hand, a cigarette burning brighter as she inhaled. She had a fake ID that said she was twenty-one. Once, she'd had me quiz her on the new facts of herself: height and weight and date of birth. She'd even memorized the license number, a long number that would only look suspicious if she rattled it off.

She sat beside me.

"You look homeless," I said.

"A homeless man bought it for me," she said, taking a swallow. "Or maybe he wasn't homeless. He had a debit card."

"Where's your ID?"

"I don't look anything like that girl." She spread her legs, nearly to a full split, and I recalled the uncomfortable positions I used to sit in as a child, when my body could easily bend itself into different shapes.

"I thought we were going to order pizza," I said.

"There's a whole counter of fried shit over there—I could go get you something. Taquitos, chicken fingers, potato logs . . ."

"That's okay."

She swiped her cigarette on the bottom of her flip-flop and tossed it into the parking lot. "Don't mess with Texas," she said.

The bald man came into view, cradling a sack in his arms.

"When I passed him in the store, he grunted at me," she said.

"What'd you do?"

"What do you think I did? I ignored him. You have to ignore them or they'll be encouraged."

The man opened his door and looked over at us before closing it. I wondered what he was saying to the woman—if they were kind to each other or if they yelled and said horrible things. They were probably on drugs, like my dead cousin. Like her, maybe they'd once had normal lives, with normal families who'd loved them and they'd just gotten off on the wrong track. Or maybe things had always been like this and they didn't know any other way. Life was mean and people were mean and there was no room for kindness.

Elise lit another cigarette and called Dan. He didn't answer, so she left him a message, said she was having a terrible, awful time. Then she checked to see what the Florida leg was doing. "Greta had a fender-bender," she said, "smashed a headlight. And everybody's giving her the finger today."

"I bet she loves that."

"Seriously, though—why are all these people so unattractive? Being religious is no excuse to be this unattractive." She passed me her phone and I looked at the woman, overweight with messy gray hair, wearing a raincoat.

"Maybe she's just unattractive and religious and the two don't have anything to do with each other," I said.

"I don't know about that."

"I'm sure there are a lot of ugly atheists out there, too."

"She could at least dye her hair—she's only like fifty or something. Or maybe forty."

"Some women don't care about being beautiful."

She looked at me like I was insane. "The agnostics have to be the best-looking group," she said. "Extremists rely too much on their extremism."

I went inside and flipped through the stations until I found *Honey, I Shrunk the Kids*. It was my favorite scene, the kids lost in the grass. They were so small a stream of dog pee was a river, a baby ant the size of a Volkswagen. They were so small, an oatmeal cream pie could sustain them for years. It was every kid's dream, like finding a house made of candy in the forest. The older boy, Little Russ, was hot, even with his eighties hair, and I wanted to sleep in a Lego while he kept watch over me. No—I wanted him to forget his guard duty and climb into the Lego with me so I could run my fingers through his soft, feathered hair.

When I went to get Elise, she was gone. The lights were off in the bald man's room and I imagined the woman straddling him while he held her hips, rocked her gently back and forth. At home, we had a set of my mother's old encyclopedias and I would read and reread the entry for Sex: "A man and a woman lie next to each other and the man places his penis inside the woman's vagina. This is usually pleasurable for both parties." It was the dirtiest thing I had access to. We didn't get the premium channels and I didn't look at porn on my computer because I might forget to clear the history. Of course I wouldn't forget, but it was possible, and I'd never live down the shame.

———

My mother looked nearly girlish with her hair loose, smiling. She gazed up at my father and he leaned down and kissed her head. Occasionally, I caught glimpses into their world and it bothered me that I could never be a part of it, that I couldn't know them in the way they knew each other. We all knew each other completely differently, in ways that would never overlap.

"Where's Elise?" my father asked.

"I think she went to the store," I said.

"What are you doing out here by yourself?" my mother asked.

"The moon is nice." We all looked up at it, big and fake-looking with clouds snaking across it. My father had a book called *We Never Went to the Moon: America's Thirty Billion Dollar Swindle* that he liked to quote from. The book alleged that the moon landing had actually taken place in Nevada, and in between shooting footage the astronauts had visited strip clubs. Elise showed me a full-page spread of an exotic dancer as evidence that our father was an idiot. It was his thing, not believing in anything but God, as if to believe in anything else—man's landing on the moon, global warming— would be disloyal.

My mother opened the door and I took off my shoes and got in bed. I watched my father take an envelope out of his bag. He unfolded the purple-and-orange prayer rug and knelt on it, facing the window. Before we'd left, he'd told us we each had to kneel on it at some point and circle our prayer needs and then he'd mail it to another family and they'd mail it to another family like a chain letter.

I'd knelt on it the first night and circled every single need: spiritual revival, devotion, monetary concerns, temptation, health and well-being, stress and anxiety, salvation.

On one side of the rug was a picture of Jesus's face. His eyes were closed, but it said if you continued to look at them, they would open. They hadn't opened for me and I wondered if they were opening for my father. I'd only glanced at them because it reminded me of standing in front of a mirror chanting Bloody Mary, something I'd done at a sleepover once that had freaked me out. It would have been horrifying if Jesus opened his eyes, same as it would have been horrifying if a Bloody Mary had appeared in the mirror. Had anyone in the history of the prayer rug seen His eyes open? And if they hadn't, and no one was ever going to, why did it say that we would?

"Call her," my mother said.

I liked the picture that popped up, Elise's face in the plywood body of a meerkat at the Atlanta zoo. It rang and rang. I hung up and tried again, but there was still no answer so I left a message, trying to make it sound like she was on the other end. But then my mother asked where she was and I had to tell her I'd left a message.

"Maybe her phone's dead," my father said. Elise was always letting her phone die. I didn't understand how peoples' phones were always dying—all you had to do was plug it in at night. Who were these people who couldn't even manage that?

"It's not dead, it's ringing," I said.

"Well, try again."

It went straight to voicemail.

My father sat at the table. "I need a pen," he said, holding out his arm to my mother. She couldn't find one and his arm stayed there, outstretched with his hand waving, while my mother dug around in her purse.

He looked at the prayer needs for a long time before circling one. I wondered which one. I didn't like that our needs were going to get all mixed up, or that he knew I'd circled all of them. He left it on the table and took his robe into the bathroom, came out a few seconds later with it on.

"Turn it to the news," he said, getting into bed.

My movie was almost over—Big Russ getting test-zapped by

the machine—but I flipped around until I came to the news, the weatherman giving tomorrow's forecast.

"I kinda miss that ole fat boy," he said, which is what he called Brett Barry, the weatherman at home.

I plugged my phone into the charger and looked at my mother. I knew we were both thinking about last summer, in Destin, Florida, when Elise left the condo and didn't come in until three o'clock in the morning. She'd come back to us so drunk she couldn't stand or speak, and my mother had undressed her and put her in the bathtub.

We slipped on our shoes and went outside.

"Let's pray real quick." She took my hands, bowed her head, and closed her eyes. She asked for His protection and compassion and guidance. She asked Him to watch over us and keep us safe. "Mother Mary—" she said.

"Mom?"

She kept her head bowed, a tight grip on my hands. She was quiet for a moment. "Elise is too beautiful and naïve, Lord," she said, and then she squeezed my hands once hard before releasing them. I wanted to be too beautiful and naïve. No one would ever apologize for me because I was too beautiful and naïve.

We walked slowly across the parking lot. It was quiet and the few lit-up rooms somehow felt lonelier than the dark ones.

Before entering the bar, my mother turned to me. I thought about the bottle of whiskey and how I'd put too much water in it. How I'd done it on purpose. My father would take one sip and ask what she'd done to his drink.

She opened the door and we stepped inside. The place was small, with a couple of video games on one side and a pool table on the other. I stood in the light of the cigarette machine and watched my mother approach the bartender. There were a dozen men, leaning and sitting around the bar, the kind of big, sad men who told a lot of jokes. There was only one other female in the place, a skinny woman playing pool with a short, tattooed guy. While taking aim, the guy met my eyes and I crossed my arms in front of my chest. I'd forgotten to put my bra back on. He took his shot, balls knocking into the pockets.

Though everyone else had noticed us, the bartender pretended not to. He was doing something below the bar I couldn't see, washing glasses or drying them. When he finally acknowledged my mother, they spoke a few words and then she walked back over and stood next to me.

"She was in here, but she's gone," she said.

"Where'd she go?"

"She left with someone. He doesn't know him."

"I bet he knows him," I said. "I bet they all know each other."

"Maybe he's just passing through."

We went outside and looked up and down the street. I felt sorry for my mother. She probably wished she was still Catholic, that she didn't have to kneel on prayer rugs or talk about the end of the world all the time.

I sat on the curb and stretched out my legs. I hadn't shaved since we'd left Montgomery, and my legs were hairy, especially around the knees and ankles, spots I always missed.

"The barstools were toilets," she said.

"Toilets?"

"Raised up on a little platform."

"I didn't notice," I said.

The door opened and we were joined by the couple that had been playing pool. I was conscious of my breasts again. I had large breasts for my frame, which I found humiliating because the boys in my class had decided large breasts weren't attractive, that *more than a mouthful's a waste.* The man lit two cigarettes and handed one to the woman. She had terrible skin, her hair in a sad ponytail.

"We're looking for my daughter," my mother said, stepping toward them.

"Good-lookin' girl?" the man said, but then he seemed embarrassed.

"About five-foot-seven, I think her hair was in a ponytail. Was it in a ponytail?" my mother asked me.

"She had it down. She was wearing a tank top with candy canes on it," I said, thinking about how pretty she looked in her tiny shorts and tiny shirt, her long arms and legs.

"She was here," he said.

"Do you know where she went?" my mother asked.

"She left with Jimmy," the woman said.

"Who's Jimmy?" I asked.

There was a pause and she said, "What do you want to know about him?"

"They should be back any minute," the man said. I looked at his arms, which were littered with tattoos—small, individual drawings like someone had doodled them in the margins of a notebook. I wanted to sit with him, have him go through them one by one. I was sure each of them meant something. Trashy people had tattoos that meant things.

"The bartender wouldn't serve her," the woman said.

"Why didn't they get beer there?" I asked, pointing to the gas station. The woman shrugged. I fake yawned, hoping she'd catch it, but she didn't. It worked best if you yawned just as you were passing someone, if the person hardly noticed you at all. I liked the idea that I could pass it to someone and they would pass it to someone else and my yawn could travel, cross state lines.

My mother started breathing heavily, like she was going to hyperventilate, and I thought I should go get my father, that he'd know what to do, but he hadn't known what to do. He'd just gotten in bed and opted out of the whole thing. She kept getting more and more upset, and the man tried to comfort her, calling her "ma'am," reassuring her that Elise would be back any minute. He told her he knew Jimmy and Jimmy was a fine guy, a good guy.

"Sit down, Mom," I said, taking her hand and pulling her down. She sat next to me, so close her legs and arms touched mine. She was unhappy with us and I wanted to do everything I could to make her stay, to keep her. There was a part of me that had always been afraid she would leave. If I behaved badly, if I wasn't good enough, she might decide we weren't worth the trouble. I felt like I had to compensate for my father and sister's behavior. I didn't know why this burden had fallen to me, why I was the one who was unable to be herself, but it had always been this way.

The couple eyed us as they smoked their cigarettes and talked about a woman named Tammy. We learned all about Tammy. Tammy had two kids and two boyfriends: one bad, one good. She'd been in rehab, prison, and, most recently, the mental hospital. Now she was out and the cycle was repeating itself. She was with the bad boyfriend, wasn't answering their calls. Her kids were going to be taken away for good. I'd always thought that bad luck turned, but some peoples' lives seemed to be one bad-luck story after another with no turn. I picked up my mother's hand. I didn't know what to do with it once I had it, so I examined it for signs of aging. It didn't look too old. The bones felt nice under the skin. I turned it over and traced her head line, her heart line; her life line was weak, tapering off mid-palm.

"Do you miss being Catholic?" I asked.

"God doesn't care where you worship him as long as you go to church."

"But Catholics are different."

"They're Christians," she said, "same as us."

"Dad doesn't think so."

"I know," she said, putting her arm around me.

"I love you."

"I love you, too," she said. We said "I love you" a lot, and it hadn't seemed like a big deal until my mother told me she'd grown up in a family that never said it. When her father died, she hadn't heard those words come out of his mouth.

I was about to go get my father when we saw the car. We watched the headlights come closer and closer and then Jimmy pulled up right in front of us and my sister got out. The man looked at us through the windshield. He was old, at least forty, and didn't look like anyone Elise would have voluntarily gone off with.

While our mother stood there with her hands at her sides, my sister dragged me into the bar; she led me to the bathroom and locked the door. The bathroom was one room with two toilets and no dividers between them. There was writing all over the walls: sketches of women's faces, penises and liquor bottles, cats and rainbows and balloons. A sentence in blue marker caught my eye: IF YOU'RE READING THIS, YOU SHOULD GO HOME NOW. And then, underneath it in big block letters, LOVE ONE ANOTHER. This struck me as hugely profound—*love one another*. It seemed so simple. I was hardly ever even nice to people because I was afraid of them. It seemed ridiculous that people might need or want my love.

A red lightbulb over the sink gave the room a creepy feel, like we were being filmed, the camera's eye turning slowly to follow our movements. It reminded me of a TV show I'd seen where seven people had been kidnapped and drugged. They awoke in separate hotel rooms on the same floor and couldn't get out of their rooms until they'd found their keys, which were taped inside their Bibles. They had to kill the other six people in order to survive.

"I just wanted to see how pissed mom is," she said.

"She's really pissed," I said. "She's really upset. Why do you have to do stuff like this?"

She pulled down her shorts and sat on one of the toilets. "Like what?"

"You're being an idiot."

"Don't call me an idiot," she said. "I'm not an idiot. *You're* an idiot."

"Mom was crying in front of those people," I said.

She was so drunk her face was taking on different shapes, the muscles bunching and flattening beneath the skin. As soon as she'd gotten her shorts up, I opened the door. The bartender was standing there with our mother behind him.

"Get out," he said, and Elise started screaming that we were leaving.

"I'm sorry," I said.

"What are you sorry for?" Elise said. "You're always apologizing for things that have nothing to do with you. Nothing has anything to do with you."

Our mother grabbed her by the arm and jerked her around, hair flying. Everyone was looking at us. They were still and quiet except for the jukebox, which was loud. It was weird, all of these trashy people looking at us like we were the trashy ones. We were solidly middle class. Our parents were college-educated.

The bartender hustled us out the door and we stood there for a second before our mother started walking. We trailed behind her like little ducks, Elise carrying her flip-flops in one hand. There was a lot of glass in the parking lot, but I didn't tell her to put her flip-flops back on. It was car-window glass, the pieces small and shimmery blue, and probably wouldn't cut her.

Elise tripped over a hunk of concrete and I linked my arm through hers. She had her face to the sky, mouth open. She pointed up at something while I dragged her along, my eyes searching out the curved and shiny glass of beer bottles. The temperature had fallen and there was a breeze. It was so nice out that I wished we were driving at night and sleeping during the day. There was nothing to say we couldn't, there were enough 24-hour gas stations to see us through, but of course my father wouldn't go for it. He didn't go for anything out of the ordinary. He liked for things to be the way they were supposed to be.

"I want that ID," my mother said.

Elise handed it over without protest and my mother slipped it in her pocket. I scanned the motel to see if any lights were on: two rooms. What were the people in those rooms doing? Watching TV? Having sex? Somehow, it was more interesting to think about what people were doing when the options had been narrowed so drastically, like I might guess correctly.

Our father was asleep, his robe in a pile on the floor and the covers at the foot of the bed. His stomach was hard and tight, like a pregnant woman's belly. Our mother sighed as she took off her shoes and shorts and replaced the covers. Elise went to the sink and guzzled water out of her hand. Then she went to the bathroom, coughed a few times, and was quiet. I got in bed and waited. After a while, I went over and put my hand on the bathroom door, leaned in. She was crying. Like our mother, she would cry if she was sad and didn't care who saw or heard her. The last time we watched *Forrest Gump*, she'd bawled shamelessly throughout the entire movie and I'd had to go upstairs and finish it in my room.

"Elise," I said.

She didn't answer.

"Elise."

"Go away."

I got back in bed. A few minutes later, she crawled in next to me and put her face close to mine. I liked to sleep on my left side and she preferred her right.

"Are you okay?" I asked.

"Yeah."

"I hate it when you cry. It makes me sad."

"There's an angel looking out for me," she said. She was so close that she could only look into one of my eyes at a time.

"What?" I asked.

"I saw my angel tonight." She waited for me to say something but I didn't want our mother to hear us. Our mother believed in angels but you weren't actually supposed to see them. It was like the prayer-rug Jesus opening his eyes. He wasn't going to and anyone who claimed he had was lying or dangerous.

"Tell me about it tomorrow," I said.

She turned her back to me. As kids we used to fight to be the one who got to sleep on their preferred side, with their leg slung over the other's hip, but that was a long time ago. I put the extra pillow between us and thought, *love one another*. It was so simple. How was I always forgetting something so simple? If Jesus's message had to be reduced to one thing, that would be it.

Soon everyone was asleep and I was awake, listening to the steady, slightly ragged breaths of my sister, the snores of my mother and father. I liked to be the last one to fall asleep, the last one to see the last thing to happen in the day.

THURSDAY

When I woke up, a weak gray light was coming in through the slit in the curtains and I knew it was too early to be awake. I checked the clock: 6:24. I'd had bad dreams, a whole series of them, but could only recall the last one. I was at a concert with thousands of people, in some kind of pit, when a structure fell on us. The dream ended like that—we were alive but knew we wouldn't make it out. The death dreams weren't that bad, though, because on some level I always knew they were dreams whereas my other bad dreams felt so real, like I was failing a class and was going to have to take it over, or one of my teeth had fallen out. It was always just one tooth, usually a bottom one, and I would search for this lost tooth and find it, attempt to stick it back into my head while blood gushed. Sometimes I glued it. I'd wake up distraught, running a finger over my slick morning teeth, and the upset feeling would hang around long enough for me to forget what it was that had upset me.

My father was usually awake first, but he was still asleep. They were all snoring now, even Elise, though my father was by far the loudest and sometimes he stopped breathing for long stretches. The word "cacophony" came to me—it was a cacophony. I rolled out of bed and went to the bathroom. On the toilet, I recalled the events of last night: Jimmy looking at me through the windshield, Elise's angel, *love one another.*

I put on my shorts, grabbed my purse, and closed the door.

It was already hot out. I should have been used to the heat, but every summer it came as a surprise; every summer I wondered if it was hotter than all of the summers that had come before. A bird flew out of a tree, its wings beating so loudly I could hear every flap. I thought about a Diet Coke and what I might eat for breakfast—a bag of sandwich cookies, if they had those, a Honey Bun if they didn't. Maybe a two-pack of strawberry Pop-Tarts. If there was only a drink machine, I'd go over to the gas station and buy some powdered doughnuts. It was what I liked best about mornings—a Diet Coke and something sweet. Elise and my mother liked the night and my father and I liked the morning.

At the bald man's room, I stopped to watch the curtains flutter above the air conditioner. And then I was leaning in, trying to hear something. I wanted to hear the woman moan.

The vending machines were next to one of the out-of-order ice machines. I opened the silver flap—yellowed, empty space. I let it slam and considered the offerings. I slid quarters and dimes into the slot and a Honey Bun fell. I had a difficult time getting it out, and when I looked up, the bald man was standing there with his bucket under one arm.

"It doesn't work," I said, tilting my purse to one side to gather more change. I picked out the silver, dropped the pennies and gum wrappers back in.

"You need money?" he asked, pulling out his billfold.

"No thanks," I said.

He held out a dollar. "Here."

"That's okay."

"It's just a dollar," he said. "Take it."

I thanked him and slipped it into the machine. The bottle clattered down. It was always the same temperature, not quite cold enough.

He was still standing there with one arm around his ice bucket, looking at me, so I asked what I always asked when I was uncomfortable—if he'd been saved.

"I'm Catholic," he said.

"My mother grew up Catholic, but she's not anymore."

"I'm not anymore, either. Have *you* been saved?"

"Of course," I said, gazing out at the parking lot like there was something there.

"Did you get dunked in a lake?"

"No, just at church."

"I like to imagine you in a lake, in a white dress."

"I think that's just on TV," I said.

"I don't go to mass anymore, except at Christmas. It gets me in the spirit, kind of like turkey at Thanksgiving. I guess I'm fair-weather, is what I'm saying, like if the Cowboys are losing, I don't watch."

I nodded, smiled.

"How old are you?" he asked.

"Fifteen."

More nodding, smiling.

"Thanks for the dollar," I said.

"Hey, wait. You got any advice for an old sinner?"

I twisted the cap off my Diet Coke. "The world's going to end," I said.

"That's not advice."

"Prepare yourself for the world to end."

He reached forward and grabbed my arm. I yanked it away, but he didn't even have a grip on it; then he took a step back and showed me his palms as if he was innocent.

He looked slowly around the parking lot before turning back to me with cold eyes. "Why are you still standing here?" he asked in a voice that was different from the one he'd used before. I took off running, my purse banging against my leg.

———

I was breathing heavily and must have looked alarmed, but my father didn't notice.

"Good morning," he said, sitting up.

"Good morning." I crawled in bed next to Elise and closed my eyes. I tried to slow my breathing, but the more I tried, the harder it became. Same as sleeping and everything else, breathing was only easy if you didn't think about it. *I will kill you,* I thought. *I will rip you limb from limb.* I imagined shooting the man and watching him die, hitting him over the head with a hammer. His blood leaking all over the pavement. It made me feel powerful.

I lay there for a long time, thinking about what I would do to the man and how I would enjoy watching him suffer, but I must have fallen asleep because when I opened my eyes my father had made coffee and the cleaning lady was pushing her cart down the bumpy concrete outside.

She stopped in front of our door and banged with a handful of keys. "Housekeeping!" she called. Elise groaned and turned over.

"We'll be out in an hour," my father called.

The woman banged again and Elise yelled, "Go away!"

There was a moment of silence and then the cart rattled on. Elise flung the covers off and went to the bathroom. She turned on the shower but didn't get in, so she must have been on the toilet. It was awful using the bathroom in a space this small. Trying to be quiet, trying not to make any noise. I'd recently found that if I sat forward on the toilet and positioned myself to miss the water, I could avoid making any sound.

I checked my King Jesus t-shirt. It was still slightly damp but I put it on. It would dry as soon as I stepped outside.

After I was dressed, my face washed and teeth brushed, I stood in front of the mirror. No one was paying any attention to me—my parents were watching the news and drinking their coffee, and Elise was still in the bathroom. I only looked at myself when no one was around. There was something embarrassing about it, like I thought I was beautiful. My nose was a little big and my skin was broken out along the jawline. My hair was wavy and hung just past my shoulders. I could never get it exactly right—if I washed it every day, it was dry and frizzy, but if I alternated days, it was greasy. My eyes were nice and my eyelashes were decently long, my teeth straight without braces. Hair, body, skin—these were the three things I had to monitor. It seemed simpler when I broke them down like this, more manageable.

I sat on my bed and turned it to *Regis & Kelly*. I waited for my father to tell me to change it back but he didn't. Kelly had been to the latest *Pirates of the Caribbean* premier and she and Regis were wearing skanky black wigs. Regis was making his usual Gelman jokes, which made me feel bad for Gelman even though it was just Regis's shtick and Gelman made a lot of money and probably had a lot of friends and a nice family, too. But something about it still made me uncomfortable. I bet in his quietest moments, right before he went to sleep in his nice bed in his nice house, he hated himself.

Elise came out of the bathroom and dug through her suitcase, one towel wrapped around her body and another around her head. She pulled her t-shirt off the hanger and went back into the bathroom.

"Save me some coffee," she called. Of course the coffee was gone; the machine only made two cups. She came out wearing the same thing she'd had on for days, blue jean shorts and her King Jesus Returns! t-shirt.

"You still stink, Jesus," she said, lifting a fistful of shirt to her face. She pronounced it Hey-soose. "How's your Jesus smell?"

"Like hamburgers," I said. "And it's wet."

"They smell like Tide," our mother said.

After our father took a quick shower and put on another of his no-iron Brooks Brothers shirts, we were back on the road.

———

He pulled off after a few exits and we got in line at a McDonald's drive-thru. There were many cars, and our parents had the usual discussion about whether it would be faster to go inside or wait it out. No matter what they decided, they would determine that it had been the wrong decision.

"I could really go for some Restaurant right now," Elise said. "Some Restaurant sure would be better than another McDonald's biscuit."

"You should get that yogurt-granola parfait," I said. "You'd like that."

"Granola has a ton of calories."

"Get the pancakes, then."

"Just order for me," she said, getting out of the car. I watched her walk inside, a man in a suit rushing to hold the door for her.

"I'm about done with her attitude," my father said.

"She hasn't been feeling well," I said.

"What's wrong with her?"

"Her stomach's been upset."

"Maybe she's coming down with a bug," my mother said.

"She needs to eat some meat," my father said. "She's not getting enough protein."

"I don't think meat has anything to do with it," I said.

Elise returned as we were pulling up to the second window. My father paid with his credit card, and I thought of him double-checking the Waffle House bill, running his finger down the column.

"Perfect timing," my mother said cheerily, taking the cups and bag as my father handed them to her.

He pulled over into a parking spot to administer his insulin shot. He took his time, opening the case, lifting his shirt and squeezing hunks of stomach to find the perfect spot. As always, he was dramatic—sighing and grunting—and the process took longer than was necessary. Then he said the prayer and our mother passed the biscuits around, doctoring our father's with jelly and wrapping a napkin around it before handing it to him. He did his usual back-up-without-looking routine and it made me want him to crash even though it would be a lot of trouble for all of us and I might even get hurt in the ordeal. I still wanted him to crash. It would be his fault. He would try to blame it on us, but we would all know it was on him and he would feel terrible about it.

We were quiet after that, eating our biscuits, not listening to the Christian radio our father liked, or the country our mother preferred. Elise liked NPR, but our father was suspicious of public radio. He called *All Things Considered, Some Things Considered,* and said the women were all lesbians. I looked at my sister, sitting Indian-style with the big plastic container of pancakes in her lap, hunks of butter melting into the squishy cakes. I hoped she'd offer them to me before they got cold.

My father took his hands off the wheel to adjust his napkin

and the car drifted off the road. He jerked the wheel back into place, making me spill orange juice on myself.

"Thanks, Dad," I said. "You just made me spill orange juice everywhere."

Elise socked me in the arm. "There's another one," she said. It was her favorite Jesus billboard, the one that asked IS HE IN YOU? in bold black letters on a white background. She had a standard response, which she whispered in my ear, "If he is, I can't feel him yet."

"You know Marshall hasn't given away any of his money," Elise said as our car began to veer off the road again.

"Dad," I said. He yanked it so hard we went into the other lane.

"It would be a nice gesture, don't you think?" she asked.

"It would be a nice gesture," I agreed. "A lot of people gave their money away—the Ultcheys and the Smiths."

"And the Sellers," Elise said. Dan was a Sellers. If the rapture didn't happen, Dan was going to be poor and wouldn't be able to help her raise the baby, or even pay for an abortion.

"Hopefully they didn't give it all away," I said.

"All of it," she said. "What's the point otherwise? To show people that you *half*-believe? That you one-quarter believe?"

"They'll be taken care of," our father said.

"But, seriously. Don't you think he should give his money away? Prove he believes what he says he does?"

"He's not required to *prove* anything," our father said.

"But he's convinced all these other people to do something he's not willing to do."

"Do you think all of this is free?" he asked, waving his biscuit around. "All the caravans and billboards? He's spent millions of dollars of his own money. They're all over the world, from Abu Dhabi to Katmandu."

I had no idea where those places were, but I recalled an episode of *Garfield* when he put Nermal in a box and addressed it to Abu Dhabi. I thought it was a made-up place.

"There's nothing here," Elise said quietly.

"I can always count on you to ask the tough questions," he said.

"I could come up with some tougher ones if you like." She popped the lid off her pancakes and smeared the butter around with a finger. I passed my wrapper up to my mother and she handed me another biscuit. I'd only asked for one, but I took it and unwrapped it. While I ate, I watched out the window: the grass was brittle and yellow; shreds of tire lined the side of the road. In the span of a minute, I saw two dead dogs and one dead armadillo. I didn't care about the armadillos, but the dogs about killed me. I mentioned it and my mother told the story of the time she ran over a turtle. I'd heard this story a dozen times—how loud the crack of its shell had been, the sick feeling that followed.

I rested my head against the window and waited for the vibration to give me a headache.

"The mileage is posted every two miles here," Elise said. "It makes me feel like we're not getting anywhere."

Our mother turned on the radio. She stopped at a station our father wouldn't like, but he didn't say anything. We listened to Kelly Clarkson and Maroon 5 and Billy Joel and he even hummed along to "Piano Man." The station was the kind that was popular now—they played what they wanted and would give you money if you could tell them how much they were giving away. The jackpot was at $2,200 when my father changed the station and I repeated this to myself, but then I remembered that they wouldn't dial our area code and maybe they only called landlines, anyway.

My father pressed SCAN and found a Christian program. The man had the pleasant, confident voice of all pastors, awful and fake, but I wanted to trust it, regardless. He told a story of a child who'd been attacked by an alligator. The boy's mother kept a tight grip on him during the struggle, which was a metaphor for parents keeping a tight grip of protection on their children as they faced life's challenges. The child had no visible scars except three little half-moons from his mother's fingernails, pulling him back from certain death. Elise rolled her eyes and I made a face even though I liked the story. There had been alligators in a dream I'd had recently, but I couldn't remember what happened. I knew why I'd dreamed of them, though—in Louisiana we'd gone to a restaurant that served fried alligator tail and my father had ordered a basket. Little nuggets he dipped into different sauces. I thought I should start writing my dreams down, taking notes; it was another part of the mission I could undertake.

"Lake Amistad," our father said, tapping the window. "Some good fishin' there, I bet." He kept glancing over, jerking the wheel. "Oh man," he said. "Look at all those boats." My father had had a boat once, but my mother put it on Craigslist without telling him. I'd stood in the carport and watched a man with a handful of cash talk him down. I rarely felt sorry for my father, but that day I'd loved him more than I'd ever loved anybody.

After that, the land grew more barren. I attempted a game of solitaire on my lap while Elise scrolled through peoples' status updates on Facebook. She told me about our cousin, one of our father's sister's kids we didn't know very well, and how he was a psychic now. Our father overheard us and asked if he was still four hundred pounds.

"I don't know," Elise said. "How would I know?"

"Because you're Facebook friends with him," I said.

"He doesn't have that many photos up—you know how ugly people use a baby picture as their profile picture? That's what he does. Wait, hold on a sec, there are testimonials. 'There's just something about Cam McKnight you can't help but gravitate towards. From Day One, I knew this was a person who was firmly grounded and yet wholly spiritual and connected to the Universe in a way few people truly are. My reading was not only spot-on but incredibly moving. You can't help but think that wherever Cam's guides are speaking to him from, it's coming straight through his heart, a heart which is immeasurable in strength and boundless in love for those who come to him seeking direction in their lives.' Wow," she said. "Do you think he wrote that himself?"

"It sounds like he cut and pasted it out of a testimonials handbook," I said.

"Totally. It's fifty dollars for a half-hour reading. Should we make an appointment?"

"That would be weird."

"You're not doing that," our mother said. "What's wrong with that kid?"

"Nothing's wrong with him," our father said, and then he brought up a few of my mother's nieces and nephews—a gay man with an apartment full of empty fish tanks, an anorexic who'd swallowed a bottle of aspirin and driven herself to the hospital.

"I'm making an appointment," Elise whispered.

My mother flipped down her visor to look at us, asked what we were doing.

"We're making our psychic reading appointments," Elise said.

"You'd better not be," she said. "Hand me your phones."

"I'm kidding."

"Hand them to me."

"Why?"

"I didn't do anything," I said.

"Well then turn 'em off and put 'em away," she said.

"Mine's been away," I said. Elise muted hers so it would stop dinging but didn't turn it off. She set it on her leg, where it continued to buzz and light up and nobody said anything.

———

Our father stopped at Wendy's without consulting us. He didn't want to go into a diner full of oddball locals any more than we did, take his chances on the chicken fried steak when he could have the square beef patty he'd come to know and love. We all liked Wendy's, except for Elise, who only liked Burger King because they had a veggie burger, but their fries were bad. Their onion rings were decent but the portions meager, even if you got a large.

Elise and I went to the bathroom. There was a line bunched up in the small space, and I kept having to move because I was blocking the hand dryer. A mother had her little girl in the handicapped stall, coaching her in a high voice: "Now wipe, now pull up your panties, now your pants, are they zipped? They're not zipped. No, you can do it yourself—you're a big girl now." Somehow, it felt like it was all for our benefit.

Elise tried to call Dan but he didn't answer.

"He doesn't want to talk to you," I said.

"He always answers my calls, even at the movie. He could be in a ditch somewhere."

"He's not in a ditch—he either lost his phone or he's avoiding you."

"How do you know?" she asked. "You've never even had a boyfriend."

"I have a cell phone. I know how cell phones work—people pick up if they want to talk to you, or they see you called and call you back."

She looked like she was going to cry, so I told her I was sure it was nothing, his phone was broken or he'd lost it. Dan was supposed to love her. He told everyone he loved her. Once he'd even told me. The two of us had been sitting together in the den, waiting for Elise to finish getting ready, and I'd stopped eating a bowl of Cap'n Crunch to listen to him tell me how great she was, how she was "his person." He had found "his person" in life early and he was one of the lucky ones. He must have been drunk. By the time he finished, my cereal was soggy and I took the bowl into the kitchen and dumped it out.

Our parents were halfway through with their hamburgers when we returned. My father handed me fifteen dollars and we got in line behind a pair of guys in work clothes, their names in cursive on their shirt pockets. They stared at Elise.

"What?" she asked, and one of them mumbled, "Nothing." The other said, *"Dang."* They inched forward, discussing secret menu items.

"You know what's funny?" I said.

"What?"

"If those guys were cute, you wouldn't be like, 'What?' You'd be glad they were looking at you."

"You're a deep thinker," she said. "One of the best thinkers of our time."

"Fuck you." The counter lady heard me and looked horrified.

I ordered a combo: cheeseburger, fries, and a vanilla Frosty— which was even better than the original—and Elise ordered a side salad and a baked potato with butter, sour cream, and chives.

"Why can't we ever go to Burger King?" she asked, taking everything off of our tray.

"Because their fries are awful," I said, unwrapping my burger. "It's like they were fried and then sat for a while and then fried again." I looked out at the parking lot, packed with cars and trucks and boats.

"Bow your heads," our father said, and we stopped eating and looked at the table. Somebody had spilled salt everywhere. My father grasped my hand so tightly I didn't have to hold his at all. My sister's hand was cool and dry.

"Dear Heavenly Father," he said.

"Why do we always have to pray in public?" Elise asked, cutting him off. "People are staring at us."

"People are always staring at you," I said. Nobody was looking at us except for a well-dressed older lady sitting by herself. She was smiling, but it was a sad smile, like she'd had a family once, too.

"We're praying because we're about to eat," our father said. "To thank Him for providing this food for us."

"You always do it so loud."

My father bowed his head and continued.

We ate in silence until Elise asked if anyone wanted her potato.

"I don't eat vegetarian food," our father said, in the nastiest voice he could muster.

"It's a potato," Elise said. "You're eating potatoes right now. You also eat eggs and grits and bread and ice cream and about a million other things that are vegetarian." She got up and threw her food away. I was worried that the baby wasn't getting enough nutrients. At home, she mixed chocolate protein powder with vanilla almond milk, took multivitamins.

She went to the bathroom again and I listened to a conversation at a nearby table—a white girl with cornrows telling her friend she didn't eat chicken. Her friend said it was un-Ameri-can. "What *do* you eat?" she asked.

"Hog, cow," the girl with cornrows said. I'd never heard any-one say "hog" or "cow" to refer to meat before.

I finished my burger and fries, saved my Frosty for later.

———

In the parking lot, a man approached my father with a story about a dead body he had to pick up in Oklahoma, and the gas money he needed to get there. My father said he didn't have much and the man told him his older brother had been in an automobile accident and there was no one else to claim him. The body had been in the morgue for three days. Elise walked over to the car. My father repeated that he didn't have much money and then asked how much he needed and the man went over the mileage there and back and said he guessed about eighty dollars. When my father hesitated, the man told him he had a check for that exact amount but didn't have time to cash it. He promised to take our address and pay us back, swore he'd have the money by Monday and could put it in the mail.

We left our father with the man, who wasn't poorly dressed or dirty. He was just a regular man, a little overweight, in worn but clean clothes. I wouldn't have given him anything, but he wasn't looking at me like that, with those eyes full of need and an answer for everything.

My mother and I got in the car. She played with the radio while Elise and I watched.

"I can't believe he's giving him money," Elise said.

"It's okay," our mother said.

"But we don't *have* any money."

"We have money."

"We know he lost his job."

"It's not your business what your father does," our mother said. "He wouldn't give it if we didn't have it to give."

"Is that true? He lost his job?" I asked, stirring my Frosty, which tasted better when it was half-melted, like a cold delicious soup.

"And now he's giving him some more!" Elise said. "Oh my God. Anybody could tell that was a story—he's been rehearsing it all day." My mother turned the air conditioner up and adjusted all the vents so they pointed at her. "If he gives that man our address, he's a bigger idiot than I thought."

Our father got back in the car, wiping his face with a handkerchief.

"How much did you give him?" Elise asked.

There was a long pause before he said, "Eighty dollars," like he couldn't believe it himself.

"Eighty dollars!" Elise said.

"He needed it more than we do."

"Did you even give him a tract?" I asked.

"He was in a bad fix," he said.

My father knew he'd been taken but stuck with his story—that he believed the man—the man wasn't on drugs or alcohol, and was clearly in a bad fix. It made me a little sick to think about his wallet minus eighty dollars. I imagined the man at the liquor store, buying steaks for a cookout. How he'd tell the story of the sucker who gave him eighty bucks and laugh.

"Did you give him our address?" I asked.

"It's bad practice to lend money, it creates resentment. Money should be given with no expectation of repayment," he said, trying to turn it into a teaching moment.

"I'm going to be sick," Elise said. "Pull over."

Our father pulled onto the big shoulder, cutting off a truck in the right-hand lane. The person in the truck laid on the horn; he honked so long we could hear it fade out. Elise toppled out of the car making retching sounds, but there was only a string of spit.

After several more hours—during which time the radio was silent and everyone slept or pretended to sleep—our father pulled off at an exit. I hadn't seen a sign advertising gas and he was taking his chances. He'd waited nearly too long. The car told him exactly how many miles it had to go until it was empty and we were down to eight, which was the lowest he'd gotten while traveling, though not in Montgomery. In Montgomery, he'd made it to two.

"You ran out of gas once," our mother said.

Elise and I didn't remember him running out of gas, but he didn't deny it. And then we were at seven miles and the car dinged again—*ding, ding, ding!* Elise raised her eyebrows at me and elbowed me for good measure.

At the top of the hill, we looked left and right and saw no sign of a gas station, no sign of anything in either direction.

"What do you think?" he asked. "Left or right?"

"Why didn't we get gas when we stopped for lunch?" my mother asked.

"That question isn't relevant or helpful, Barbara," he said. He never called her Barbara. It was funny hearing her name.

"It might not be helpful but it's certainly relevant, *John*," she said.

"Take a right," I said.

"That means left," Elise said. "Jess has a one hundred percent inaccuracy rate."

"That's true," I said. "I do."

He took a left and drove a ways and then a ways farther. He was searching for a place to turn around when we saw it. The gas station sat by itself, weeds growing up through chunks of concrete. There were bars on the windows and the advertisements were all in Spanish. It was hard to believe that there was any need for a gas station out here.

"I bet the bathroom's on the outside," Elise said. "I hate when it's on the outside."

"I like those enormous keys," I said.

Our father went inside to pay—the pumps didn't take credit cards—and the three of us followed him. Two men stood in front of a fireplace, smoking and drinking coffee. It was like we'd walked into their living room. They stopped talking and one of them pointed to the right back corner.

Elise tried the knob and it opened, felt around for the light. She shut the door, but then she opened it and pulled me inside with her.

"I think it's a front," she said. "There wasn't much for sale."

"Gas is for sale," I said.

"It's a front," she said, "trust me. I know one when I see one."

The bottle of soap had been diluted to a thin pink liquid. I pumped some into my hands and held them under the water while Elise squatted over the toilet. There wasn't a mirror. There wasn't even the outline of a place a mirror had been.

"I hate traveling," she said. "People think it's so fun to be uncomfortable but it's not fun. I'm not feeling *challenged*. I'm not *learning* anything."

"Who thinks it's fun to be uncomfortable?"

"Oh you know, traveler types. On the upside, at least my period won't be making a surprise appearance."

"That's not funny."

"You're right," she said. "It's not funny. It's not funny at all. Hand me a paper towel, this toilet paper is wet."

Our mother and father were waiting when we opened the door.

"Use the paper towels," I said.

Elise told the men that the bathroom needed toilet paper and they nodded slowly. We debated over popsicles, deciding coconut would make us feel like we were on vacation. We opened the wrappers and placed them on the counter, ate them while checking out the bricks of beige candy, bags of chips with crazy fonts. I picked up a thick bar with almonds on top and Elise took it out of my hand and put it back.

"Mexican candy isn't any good," she said. "It just tastes like sugar."

"I like sugar."

"It tastes like stale old sugar. Let's look at the shirts."

We flipped through a rack of oversized t-shirts in thick, scratchy cotton until Elise noticed a stack of cowboy boots in a corner.

"Dude," she said. "I can feel it. It's my lucky day."

She sorted through the boxes until she found a pair of bright blue boots in her size. She held her popsicle between her teeth as she slipped one on. "A little big," she said, turning her foot this way and that. She put her hands on her hips. "What do you think?"

"They make your legs look good."

"They do, don't they?" she said, kicking a Styrofoam cooler.

Our father came out of the bathroom and I waved. When I saw him in public, even at an empty gas station in the middle of nowhere, I liked him better. I thought about these men treating him unkindly or laughing at him and it hurt my feelings.

Elise put her flip-flops in the box and placed it next to our popsicle wrappers, and our father paid without comment. Once we were in the car, I wished I'd gotten a pair so we would be wearing the same thing, but I hadn't even checked to see if they'd had my size.

———

Our mother wanted to stop at a flea market in a dusty town full of cactuses and oversized aloe vera plants. "It's one of the top-ten flea markets in the country," she said. "And it's on the highway we're already on so we won't even have to go out of our way."

"We could pass out tracts," Elise said.

"Like you would ever pass out tracts," I said.

"I've passed out tracts before."

"When?"

"You know, that time," she said. "At that thing."

From the highway, it didn't look like much—a wide gravel lot and some makeshift buildings attached to other makeshift buildings, a few tents scattered around the edges. Our father parked and we all got out, our eyes adjusting to the brightness.

"Take some tracts," he said, and I put a few in my purse.

At home the flea market our mother frequented was full of old people selling junk from their attics: stamps and clothes and Christmas decorations, porcelain dolls in yellowed dresses—the same things week after week that nobody seemed to buy, or else they had an unlimited supply. But this was a Mexican flea market, full of Mexicans, my father pointed out, but he got excited when we passed the first concession stand selling turkey legs and funnel cakes for two dollars apiece.

He bought a huge Coke and a funnel cake and we strolled the aisles, looking back and forth between the booths of refurbished washing machines, VHS tapes and serving dishes, cowboy boots and cowboy hats, and so many baby things: baby clothes and baby toys and baby strollers and baby bassinets. I watched Elise to see if her eyes lingered on any of it. Maybe she would pick up a tiny pale pink dress and it would change everything.

I stopped in front of a big-butted mannequin wearing an off-the-shoulder dress. They waited as I sorted through the rack and chose a shirt with Our Lady of Guadalupe on the front. It was gaudy, something I'd never wear at home. I paid for it and put it on over my King Jesus t-shirt, and we continued walking, pulling pieces off of our father's funnel cake until he passed me the plate and bought himself a turkey leg. He was so happy with his turkey leg, wiping his mouth with the back of his hand.

I watched an older woman in a tight black jumpsuit put on mascara, her mouth an O and her eyes wide. She was looking in a mirror and didn't care who stopped, mid-aisle, to gape at her. Her booth was selling miscellaneous electronics, VCRs and cassette players, things that had become obsolete.

Our mother detoured into a pottery booth and our father stopped. Elise and I kept walking, men forming a loose circle around us, talking to each other in rapid Spanish. A teenager swept the pavement in front of us while we pretended not to notice. I dared her to say something to him, thought it would scare him if she actually spoke.

"I wonder if they'll sell us a margarita," she said, digging around in her purse. "Give me some money."

"You have money."

"No, I don't," she said.

"You can't drink here, anyway."

"The drinking age is eighteen in Mexico."

"We're in Texas."

"I know we're in Texas but do you see any white people?" she asked, but then she became distracted by a man drawing a caricature of two teenage girls. Next to the man, a sad woman in full-on tiger face sat at a card table. Her sign said, SMALL DESIGN

$4 WHOLE FACE $9. She had a boy haircut and was wearing regular clothes. I wondered why someone would paint her face like a tiger and drive all the way out here to sit at a card table, looking so miserable that no one would ever go near her.

"Maybe we should get our faces painted," I said, nodding at the woman. "Or just go over there and talk to her. Drum up interest."

"She's so sad," Elise said.

"I know. It's making me sad."

"Don't ask her if she's been saved."

"I'm not going to ask her that," I said. "I don't ask people that anymore."

"Since when?"

"Since now."

The woman's head turned toward me, so slowly that I had time to look back at the drawing of the two girls without getting caught. In real life, one of the girls was fat and the other was thin, but in the drawing they were the same size. The thin girl, however, was given sexy eyes with long eyelashes.

Our mother and father shuffled past. Our father was still working on his turkey leg, and our mother was smiling and looking about excitedly.

Elise approached the tiger woman, who didn't acknowledge her until she sat across from her in the blue plastic chair. I went over and stood next to my sister.

"We both want full face," Elise said.

"I was thinking smaller," I said.

"Full face. What can you do besides tigers?"

"Zebras, lions—" the woman said.

"I'm not feeling very safari animal today," Elise interrupted.

"Elf, mermaid, Smurf, cow, snake, chimpanzee," the woman continued.

They decided on a snake, its mouth open wide above one eye.

"See, you *do* like snakes," I said.

Her snake was awful, a coral snake or the snake that looks like a coral snake but isn't poisonous. When it was finished, the woman held up a mirror and Elise said it was amazing.

"I want the tiger," I said, sitting down in the seat Elise had warmed for me. The woman stared at me with no expression whatsoever—it didn't seem to please her like I'd imagined it would—and picked out the colors.

Her fingers were cool, papery. I liked the feel of them on my cheek.

"How long have you been doing this?" I asked.

"Awhile," she said.

"Do you get much business?"

"Sometimes," she said. "It's been slow lately."

"The recession," I said, like I knew what I was talking about. I had heard talk of this recession for years. I must have been born in a recession.

There was something about the face-painting woman that made me achy. It felt a little like love, though I'd never been in love and couldn't say for sure what it was. I wondered if it would always feel like pain.

Elise wandered off and I watched the men gather.

"Do you live nearby?" I asked.

"Not far," she said. "A few miles."

She didn't have a ring on her finger. I could nearly always predict who would have a ring on their finger. If they were young, they were usually pretty and had positive attitudes. The ones I would want to marry myself if I had to marry a woman. They would drag you out of bed in the morning and say what a nice day it was, even if you were sick or sad or it was raining and you'd get up and do things and feel better. They'd make lunch and dinner, put clean sheets on the bed.

I concentrated on her fingertips pressing into my cheek. *Just feel this. There is only now.* I kept telling myself to be in the present, which kept me from being in the present. I wanted her fingers on my face forever, or at least a very long time.

She handed me the mirror, and I hesitated long enough for her to know that whatever I said next wouldn't be the truth. "I love it," I said. I had the urge to wash it off immediately. I paid her and then took out my phone and snapped a picture of her next to her sign.

"You didn't ask if you could take her picture," Elise said. "Maybe she didn't want her picture taken."

"What?"

"You should always ask first."

"It's not like this is a third-world country and she's naked and covered with flies."

"You should always ask."

"Back off," I said. I saw our parents turn a corner, and we ran to catch up with them.

"What'd you buy?" I asked my mother.

"What's all this?" our father said. He had another funnel cake, a fresh hot one. Powdered sugar caked at the corners of his lips. Elise told him about the woman we'd met, a sad woman whose spirits we'd lifted by having our faces painted.

"Was she saved?" he asked.

"Yes," I said. "I gave her a tract anyway."

My mother showed me her purchases—two soap dishes and a delicate gold bracelet. My father stopped at a covered pavilion with a lot of tables. He sat at one and I sat across from him. My mother and Elise kept walking.

A band was setting up, a Mexican band in Mexican costumes. I looked at my shirt, felt the paint on my face. I was in disguise.

"How are you?" he asked after a while.

"Good," I said, stealing glances at his cake.

"Are you having fun?"

"Yeah, I'm having a good time." I had a friend at school, more of an acquaintance really, who was always asking everybody how they were feeling. "*How are you feeling?*" she'd ask, because someone had labeled her the caring friend. I always told her I was fine, but what would she do if I said I wasn't fine? Next time she asked, I was going to tell her I was terrible and see what happened.

The band began to play a traditional Mexican song, the kind of song that sounded like every other song, but maybe it didn't to the Mexican ear. Maybe it was like the faces of a different race, how it was harder to tell them apart. I wondered if they'd play "La Bamba" but figured they only played it for white people. Once I'd decided they weren't going to, I really wanted to hear it.

"I need a picture of you in that getup," my father said.

I got out my phone and tapped the camera button. "Just press here," I said, passing it across the table. I noticed the number 2 on his hand over yesterday's faded 3. He took my picture, shook his head a little, and smiled.

"Are you hungry?" he asked.

"No, I'm good," I said. He was trying so hard and I wanted to give him something but couldn't. I felt totally incapable of it.

"Your mother's worried about you."

"Why?"

"You've been mighty quiet."

"I'm fine," I said. "We've all been pretty quiet."

"Not Elise."

"She doesn't know how to be quiet," I said.

I reassured him that everything was fine as the band played the first few notes of "La Bamba." What did he want me to say? He always asked such big questions, questions that there was no way for me to answer.

"Why don't you go tell them we're ready?" he said, wiping his hands on a crumpled napkin.

I went. My mother had made a few more purchases, her hands full of bags. I took them from her and we met my father at the car.

———

We drove for hundreds of miles with nothing to see but a bunch of low, craggy mountains. Mostly they were in the distance, and didn't seem to be getting any closer, but then I'd look up and we'd be driving through slices of smooth stone.

"Is there a map of Alabama somewhere?" Elise asked.

My father pulled the stack of maps from his car door and sorted through them, his other hand moving back and forth on the wheel like somebody driving on TV. Our mother reached out to steady it and he waved her hand away.

He found the map and passed it back, and Elise looked up the elevations of our mountains so we could compare them to the ones in Texas, but there was no comparison—the mountains in Texas were six times the size of ours.

We drove through a series of small towns, one of them an actual ghost town. Sanderson was by far the most desolate place I'd ever seen: dirt and power lines and signs advertising propane, a Kountry Kitchen restaurant. There were a few two- and three-story buildings right next to the highway, buildings that could have held a lot of people, but none of them appeared to be open and there were few cars in the lots. Elise got out her phone and started filming. She tried to talk our father into stopping so we could walk around, but he said we were done stopping. We were behind schedule.

"What schedule?" she asked.

"You know what schedule," I said. "California."

"I'm still not sure why we're going there," Elise said. "Why are we going there?"

"You know why," I said.

"Remind me."

"Because that's where Marshall is," I said.

"It's not like we're going to meet him."

"We might," I said.

"That's not the reason we're going to California," our father said.

"Then why are we going?" Elise asked.

"Because it's in Pacific Time," I said.

"I'm not asking *you*. I'm asking *Dad*."

"We're preparing," I said.

"Shut up, Jessica," she said. Nobody called me Jessica. I didn't like the sound of it. It had too many syllables. "Dad?"

"We're on a pilgrimage," he said calmly, but his ears and neck were red and he was shaking.

I watched him fade back to his normal color and thought about how he'd sold the trip to us in the first place. We were at home, eating my mother's meatloaf and my father's cornbread, when he'd pitched the idea: a pilgrimage to California. We didn't need a caravan—we could be our own caravan. And hadn't we always wanted to see the country? I'd wanted to go to Disney World as a kid, and I'd wanted to see some caves once, after watching a program about Mammoth Cave, but we only went to Destin year after year because one of my mother's sisters had a condo there.

As the trip had been over a month away, I agreed easily. It was easy to agree to things when nothing was required of me at the moment, or in the very near future. I regretted it later, of course, when getting out of the thing I had agreed to was much more difficult than not having agreed to it in the first place, but I knew this wasn't like that. If my father wanted to go to California, we would go. If he wanted a pilgrimage, we would be his pilgrims. Our mother reminisced about a cross-country trip she had taken as a child. It was a story I'd heard many times, all centering around one bathroom stop in which her father had embarrassed them, and the geysers at Yellowtsone. It was like she had no memory at all, like she'd taken photographs so there'd be no need to recall the actual event. Elise was the only one to resist, saying she had cheerleading practice and might need to retake a class. When that didn't persuade him, she said, "*The last shall be first and the first shall be last,*" but this seemed to strengthen his argument. We would wait our turns, he said.

I looked out the window. There was no grass, no trees. My father drove faster and faster, the land so barren it was easy to imagine the world had already ended and we hadn't heard.

———

"These are some of the least populated counties in the country," our father said, breaking the silence.

Elise's phone beeped and she smiled at it. Then she leaned over and said, "Dan dropped his phone in the lake. He had to get a new one."

"I told you," I said, though it didn't explain why he hadn't emailed her, or why he hadn't borrowed someone else's phone to call her. Any one of his friends would have had her number.

She touched her hair, as if to remind herself she was beautiful.

"I told you he wasn't in a ditch." I scratched at my tiger face, getting yellow paint in my fingernails. "Which lake?"

"I don't know *which lake*," she said, and stopped typing to give me a dirty look.

They spent the next half-hour texting. I wanted to text someone but no one was expecting to hear from me. I had friends but they were mostly school or church friends. We didn't play with each other's hair or tell each other our deepest secrets. It wasn't at all what I'd thought junior high friends would be like—I thought we'd be sleeping in the same bed, shopping for clothes. I thought we'd tell each other everything. I knew it was my own fault. When someone lightly touched my arm or leg while we were talking, I flinched. I didn't know how I could want things so badly while making it impossible to ever get them.

In Valentine, we insisted on stopping so we could get a snack.

I went to the bathroom—my tiger was all smeared and there were little trails of flesh peeking out. I washed it off, the paint leaving behind a sticky yellow film.

I bought a package of gummy bears—250 calories, no fat— and Elise bought a bag of popcorn, a giant pickle, and a Sprite. She never drank Sprite because it had a lot of calories, and I took it as a sign that she was starting to think about the baby.

"A little old for face-painting, aren't you?" the man behind the register asked Elise.

"I still trick-or-treat, too," she said.

I thought about Elise's Halloween costumes: she was always a dead slutty something, same as her friends. She seemed too cool to be a dead slutty something but she wasn't.

Back in the car, I ate all of the red gummy bears first, followed by the orange and yellow, and then the white and green. I

poked my mother and dropped my empty wrapper into her lap.
She opened her eyes and turned to me.

"Do you have a headache?" I asked. She liked to call them
cluster headaches because it made them sound more ominous.
She said they were very serious and that more than 20 percent of
the people who got them killed themselves.

"I'm just resting," she said. "I didn't sleep well last night."

"Me either."

"I'm sorry," she said, squeezing my hand.

———————

We usually stopped by four o'clock, but my father drove past
four o'clock and past five o'clock. We grew antsy, counting down
the miles to towns that quickly came and went. Finally, he took
an exit for a rest station.

We got out and stretched, looked around. The vending
machines were protected by bars.

"Not even the vending machines are safe here," I said, but no
one laughed. The rest stop was pretty nice, actually—the lawn
was freshly mowed and there was a fountain. People walked
their dogs.

My mother, Elise, and I went into the bathroom.

"Men have sex in rest-stop bathrooms," Elise said. "I read an
article. They call them something—I forget what they call
them."

"You're always filling your mind with trash," our mother
said. "If you fill your mind with trash, that's what you'll think
about."

"You mean if you fill your mind with trash, you'll be trash," I said. I was in the middle stall, could see their feet on either side.

"That's not what I mean," my mother said.

"That's exactly what you mean," said Elise. "You think we're trash."

"Don't bring me into it," I said. "I'm not trash."

Our mother got her feelings hurt, said we were always assuming things, putting words into her mouth.

Elise and I bought Cokes at the vending machines and sat beside the fountain, tapping our flip-flops on the water. First she'd tap, making ripples, and then I'd tap. When we grew tired of that, we made wishes. We tossed in our pennies first, one at a time, and then our nickels, dimes, and quarters.

"Van Horn's coming up," our father said, walking up behind us. "We'll stop there."

"That sounds like a good place," I said for something to say. So much of what he said required no response, but if no one said anything, his words just hung there. He gave us the coins from his pockets and we threw those in, too, but after a while I realized I'd stopped wishing and was just throwing.

———

Van Horn, Texas, was a tiny dot on the map.

Our father pulled into the crappiest motel we'd stayed in yet, sprawling and one-story, painted in hospital blues and greens.

"Things are steadily going downhill for this family," Elise said. This struck us as funny and we laughed.

"We're on a budget," our father said. "How about I get you your own room? How about that?"

"That would be nice," Elise said.

"I don't know if that's a good idea," our mother said.

"It'll be fine," Elise said. "I won't let Jess out of my sight."

Our father got out of the car looking beaten, and I started to get that crushing feeling again, like my whole body was welling up, but then it went away and I was just irritated and hot.

While we got our luggage, a man on a bicycle cruised around us in wide circles. His pants were so short his skinny brown calves showed. One of his irises was whitish, terrifying. He rang his bell, nearly losing his balance, and my father pulled a tract out of the trunk. We must have had a thousand of them, stashed all over.

"Hey," he called, flapping it back and forth at him. The man looked alarmed and circled wider before pedaling off.

"I bet this place is full of hookers," Elise said.

"I don't see any hookers," our mother said.

"That's because they're all busy."

My father handed me some tracts. Then he took the cooler out and opened the plug to let the water drain.

"I feel like I haven't handed out tracts in forever," I said.

"Speak for yourself," he said. "I handed out dozens yesterday."

"I can't remember yesterday," I said. "I'm losing track of my days—what day is it?"

"Thursday," Elise said.

Our father gave us each a key and said he loved us and we

said we loved him, too. Then we kissed our mother and told her we loved her.

I slipped tracts under windshield wipers as we went.

"People are going to hate you," Elise said.

"Maybe somebody'll read it," I said.

"No one's going to read it, it's just going to piss them off."

I inserted my key and pulled it out; the light blinked red. I tried again and got the same thing.

"You never do it right—there's a technique. You have to put it in real slow and hold it there a second before pulling it out." She winked at me and opened the door. We set our keys and purses on the table.

"This is the kind of place people kill themselves in," she said, and I thought about our wholesome-looking cousin—she hadn't killed herself, she'd been *murdered*. It seemed impossible. In all of the pictures and videos I'd seen of her, she'd looked normal, just a regular girl, like me but prettier.

"Maybe we're out of money," I said.

"Well, *yeah*, but we have credit cards and that's what they're for, so we don't have to stay in motels with bike thieves and hookers," she said. "I think he's trying to teach us a lesson, but I'm not sure what it is."

"Maybe they're maxed out," I said, unwrapping the thin bar of soap.

"He's been using them," she said.

"Maybe they're *almost* maxed out." I brought the bar to my nose—it smelled spicy. I washed my face again, trying to get the yellow tint off. Then I sat in bed while she plucked her eyebrows. She told me I ought to start plucking mine, that they were getting out of control.

"Are you gonna wash that thing off your face?" I asked, digging around in my ear. I scraped out something that felt like a bug but was just the crust of a tiny scab I hadn't known was there.

"I like it."

"It makes you look insane."

"Take a picture first," she said, tossing her phone onto my bed. I took a picture of her posed against the wall, making some sort of gang sign.

While she washed her face, I turned on the weak light and went through the contents of my bag. I refolded a couple of tank tops, counted the number of clean panties I had left. I was going to have to start washing them in the sink.

Elise stripped down to her bra and panties.

"Put your clothes back on," I said.

"Why?"

"I don't want to see you." She seemed hurt, so I said, "You're too pretty—it makes me feel bad."

"Don't say that."

"Why?"

"I don't like when people compliment my looks."

"How come?"

"I don't know," she said. And then, "Because it reminds me that I'm going to die. If someone says I have nice teeth, I think, *One day they'll rot*. If they say I have nice hair, I think about it falling out by the fistful."

"I'd love it if people told me I was pretty. I'd trade it for smart or talented or anything else."

"That's stupid," she said.

"You would, too."

"No I wouldn't."

"You don't know," I said. "You have no idea."

"Let's go to the pool." She unhooked her bra and I turned my head. There was a baby in her flat, tan stomach. I pictured it fully formed, a perfect little girl that looked exactly like her except for one thing—the eyes or nose of someone else. "You see this triangle here?" she asked, sticking a finger in the empty space below her vagina. Her pubic hair was shaved nearly to nothing. "Factory air. It's Dan's favorite part of me."

"Who calls it that?"

"I don't know, boys."

"Where'd it come from?" I asked.

"I have no idea," she said.

"Look it up on Urban Dictionary."

She picked up her phone and typed while I waited. "'The space created between a woman's thighs when she's standing with her legs parallel to each other, and perpendicular to the floor. As in, Dude, that chick had some nice factory air. I bet she doesn't ever get any duck butter.'"

"What's duck butter?"

"It just occurred to me—his favorite part of me is a part that doesn't exist."

My phone signaled the arrival of a text message and I dug it out of my purse. Nobody had called or texted me in days. One time my cell phone rang and Elise said, 'That's what your ring-tone sounds like?' as if I hadn't had the same one for a year. The text was from an unknown number in our area code. *Bitch*, it said. It made my heart drop and I looked around the room as if the person could see me. I thought about who might have a rea-son to call me a bitch and came up with no one. It was the wrong number but I couldn't help taking it personally. *Bitch*, I thought. *I'm a bitch.* I deleted it without telling Elise, who was down on the floor doing pushups, asking me how her form was.

―――――――

We put on our swimsuits and the too-short dresses we only wore to the pool, and walked around to the fenced-in area. We claimed a couple of chairs, draped the tiny motel towels over the backs of them. I stepped out of my flip-flops, nearly losing my balance. Elise looked natural out of her clothes but I didn't; it was my attempt to look natural more than anything that made me so awkward. I felt like my limbs had been taken off and reat-tached in different positions.

Once we were settled, we turned our attention to the three boys drinking beer at a table. They were listening to the radio. The station played Nirvana and The Doors and Elise started naming all of the rock stars she could think of who had killed themselves or OD'd at twenty-seven.

"That guy from Sublime," she said. "What was his name?"

"I've never heard of Sublime," I said.

"But maybe he wasn't twenty-seven, I'm not sure. Do you know Blind Melon? You know Blind Melon, right?"

"No."

"That song about the rain, with the bee? How's it go?"

"I don't know it," I said, watching a father and son in the pool—the boy was learning how to swim. "Let's just do it one more time," the father kept saying, and the boy was trying everything—he was tired, he had a stomachache—and then he was bawling. I looked over at the table of guys and the blond caught my eye. It forged some kind of bond between us. And then the blond and his friend were out of their chairs, walking over to us.

Elise lifted her sunglasses and said, "Hi, y'all," in a ridiculous accent.

"You guys aren't from here," said the blond.

"That's right," she said.

"We're from Montgomery," I said. "Alabama. We don't really talk like that." I smiled and he smiled back. It was crooked and made his eyes disappear. Unlike nearly everyone, he was more attractive when he wasn't smiling. They introduced themselves as Erik and Gabe, and said they had a cooler full of beer if we wanted to join them.

"Maybe in a minute," Elise said, her voice normal again.

They went back to their table and their other friend laughed and tossed a can at them. It went into the pool and the father threw it back.

"We don't have to go over there," she said. "They're clearly assholes."

"I kind of liked the blond."

"Just listen to them," she said. They were laughing, probably at nothing. No matter how smart boys were, they always seemed so dumb.

"We don't have anything better to do, and the blond's cute."

"Okay," she said. "But you don't have to drink."

"I know."

"Drinking doesn't make you cool."

"Am I in a public service announcement right now?"

"That's funny, a public service announcement."

I stood and slipped on my dress. "Weren't you the one feeding me straight whiskey last night?" I asked.

"There was ice in it." She kept lying there, her ribs and pelvic bones on display, the baby hidden neatly inside. I couldn't stop thinking about it—how no one knew, no one could see. If I hadn't found the box, if she hadn't wanted me to find it, I wouldn't know.

She waited a minute before following me over to their table.

"Hey, girl," the blond said to me—Gabe. His hair was so pale it was nearly white, his chest smooth and muscular. The popular boys in my class were scrawny; it wasn't cool to go to the gym. It wasn't cool to appear to be trying to be anything.

The boy we hadn't met introduced himself as Charlie and got up to grab another chair while Erik passed around beers. They were so cold and everybody was so good-looking I felt like I was in a commercial. I pretended to take an interest in the father and son. The father was swimming laps while his kid sat on a step. I wondered if his mother was waiting in one of the rooms, but more than likely his parents were divorced and the man only had his son a few weeks every summer. To make things exactly even, they drove the same number of miles and exchanged him in the middle, which happened to be this shitty little West Texas town. It would explain why they were so disappointed in each other.

Elise took a Marlboro out of somebody's pack and lit it with her bedazzled lighter before any of the boys could reach for their Zippos. I pressed my finger into a tiny flower on the table. It stuck and I thought about making a wish, but I'd been making a lot of wishes lately and they were the same generic wishes I always made. I was going to have to start being more specific. *Gabe,* I thought, blowing it off. *I want Gabe.*

"What are you guys doing here?" Charlie asked.

"We're going to California where we're going to witness the Second Coming of our Savior, the Lord Jesus Christ. In Pacific Time," Elise said. She told them we were the chosen ones, that they were going to suffer through terrible fires and earthquakes before the earth exploded into nothingness.

"Stop," I said.

"What?"

"You're making a joke out of us."

"I'm not making us a joke," she said. "I'm making *them* a joke."

"But we're here, too."

"We're kids," she said. "All we can do is act like jerks."

"You do a good job of that," I said.

She blew smoke past my face, rolled her eyes.

"She believes in it," Elise said, and the boys looked at me with half-smiles.

"I don't know if I do or not," I said. "I might be agnostic." I liked the way it sounded. I took a sip of beer, which tasted a little less awful than it usually did because it was so cold. Like Elise, I sat in church and felt nothing. I memorized Bible verses same as I did Robert Frost poems in school. But I wanted to believe. I really wanted to. If the rapture was coming, I hoped our parents' belief would be enough to get us into heaven, like Noah, whose family had been saved because he was a good man.

Charlie opened another beer, placing his empty on the stack. "Every group has its own eschatology," he said.

"Its own what?" I asked.

He took off his sunglasses so we could see his eyes. "It's how we deal with death," he said. "It's human nature to want the world to end when we end."

"Hey, girl," Gabe said, "you want another?"

"Keep 'em coming," I said, though my beer was still half-full. I liked how he called me *girl*, as if there were too many girls to remember, as if the names of girls would take up too much space in his head. If he liked me, maybe I could become *pretty girl* or even *my girl*. But for this to happen, we'd have to fast-forward past all of this getting-to-know-you business. We'd have to pretend we already knew each other. People were so similar once you got to know them.

I watched him out of the corner of my eye, his body in constant motion—an ankle bouncing on a knee, his hand lifting a can to his mouth. I wanted to feel his body move over mine. Before leaving home, Elise and I had watched a religious documentary that was streaming on Netflix. In it, all of the girls said that they very much wanted the rapture to come, but would prefer if it waited until they had husbands. They didn't say *sex*. They said *marriage, husband*. They said their parents had gotten to marry and have children and they only wanted the same opportunity.

"He should take that kid home," Gabe said, gesturing to the man, who was holding onto the side of the pool and kicking, telling the boy how easy it was.

"I know, right?"

"I didn't learn how to swim until I was fourteen," he said.

"Really?" I took a larger swallow than I'd intended, and it sat there, pooled at the back of my throat, before I could make myself choke it down.

"My dad died in a boating accident when I was two and my mom was afraid of water after that. She thought I'd drown if I went anywhere near it." This story made me think he could love me. He wasn't just a cute boy—he had problems.

"I'm sorry," I said.

He shrugged and said it was okay. "Do you know how to swim?"

"I was on the swim team at the country club for years," I said. It was actually only two years because my grandfather stopped paying our dues and we couldn't afford it after that.

"The country club," he said, "how fancy."

"Not really. It was the old people country club. My grandparents golfed there and made us eat Sunday dinner with them every week."

"You any good?"

"No," I said, laughing. "I only got pink and purple ribbons."

"I didn't even know they had those."

"I was a little better at relay. I swam so hard because I didn't want to let anybody down."

Elise opened another beer, lit one cigarette off another. She was unhappier than I'd seen her since the trip began, which was saying something. I wondered if she didn't like seeing me have fun, if she didn't want to see me happy.

"Come on," Gabe said.

I took off my dress and we walked over to the deep end. There was a NO DIVING sign, a shadow man hitting his head with an x over it, but Gabe dove in anyway and came up, flinging the hair off his forehead with a flick of his neck. Boys made every-thing look easy; it made me love them and hate them at the same time. I jumped in straight so I wouldn't make too much of a splash, touched the bottom, and pushed up hard. The father switched to breaststroke and swam around us.

I wanted Gabe to know I could take him or leave him, so I swam to the shallow end and floated on my back, watching a big gray military plane fly low overhead; low-flying planes always made me think a bomb was about to be dropped, though I'd seen hundreds if not thousands of planes and a bomb had never been dropped. It was awful being a girl. All I could think about was whether he thought I was pretty, and if he thought I was pretty, how pretty. I'd only kissed one boy, a guy I'd met at church camp who hadn't known that boys at school didn't like me. That more than a mouthful's a waste. He'd written me emails for months after, but they hadn't said anything: the places he'd gone; the things he'd eaten; what song he was learning to play on the guitar. I'd wanted to like him but couldn't, even though he was the only boy who'd ever taken an interest in me.

"Hi," I said to the kid. He picked up his head and blinked. He was only seven or eight and already had dark circles under his eyes like an insomniac. He was so sad and ugly, I didn't feel sorry for him any more.

"It looks like your kickboard got attacked by a shark," Gabe said.

The kid's father stopped swimming and looked at us like we might try something crazy. Then he took the boy's hand and hauled him out of the pool. I felt sorry for the kid again. He couldn't help being ugly—no one *wanted* to be ugly. Sometimes I had to remind myself.

When they were gone, Gabe held up his hand and I slapped it, a nice solid connection as opposed to the half-misses I usually managed. He dove under and pulled my legs, the water giving him courage he wouldn't have had on land. I came up laughing and then went under again to smooth back my hair. I wondered what his friends thought of me, if they thought I was fat. But when I glanced over at the table, they weren't paying any attention to us. They were trying to engage Elise in conversation, trying to make her laugh.

All Gabe knew about Alabama was "Sweet Home Alabama," a song that Elise and I hated because we'd had to hear it every day for our whole lives and we would continue hearing it unless we moved far away and never went back. "'In Birmingham, they love the govna,'" he sang.

"Please stop."

"That's your state song," he said. "You should have some state pride."

"Like y'all have in Texas?" I said, throwing my arms around him.

"That's right," he said.

I was having a great time until I caught my sister's eye, and then I was embarrassed. And then I was angry for being embarrassed, for always having to be the person she knew.

Elise and the other boys got into the pool with us. After less than a minute, Erik suggested we take off our tops and Gabe told him to go fuck himself and pointed out that I had on a one-piece and Charlie said I could take the whole thing off. Elise got out and put her dress on, lit another cigarette. They insisted they were kidding, only joking.

"Let's go," she said.

"You can go," I said, wrapping my legs around Gabe's waist. No wonder people liked to drink—you didn't have to be who you were, *you could change who you were.* I ran my fingers through his wet, clumpy hair. There was a pimple on his neck and I made note of its location so I wouldn't look at it again. "If I don't get raptured, will you come for me?" I asked.

"What? Like if you're left behind?"

"Yeah."

"I thought you were agnostic," he said.

"Exactly. I haven't ruled anything out."

"Well, it's a lot to ask, but okay."

"You promise?"

He placed his hand over his heart with a smack. "I'll cross the Mojave."

"What else?"

"I'll ford the Mississippi," he said. "And the Nile. The Nile, too."

"That's amazing."

"I know, I'm pretty amazing."

"Did you know that the Nile is the longest river in the world? It runs through ten African countries," I said. These were the kind of useless facts I retained. Whenever I demonstrated my knowledge, I did it like this, without weaving it into the conversation at all. I pushed off of him and floated on my back, staring up at the huge cloud blocking the sun. The rays shot out in straight thick lines like a child's drawing.

"Jess," Elise said.

I swam over to the side and held on to the ladder. "Why are you doing this?" I asked. It was nearly dark and she was far enough away that I couldn't differentiate her pupils from her irises.

"Do I need to go get Dad?" she said.

I swam back to Gabe, held onto him, and put my wet cheek against his.

"You better go," he said.

"She won't get my dad," I said. "She's just being a bitch."

He whispered "room 212" in my ear and got out. I treaded water and read the POOL RULES. No cutoffs. No glass containers, food, or drinks. No smoking. No running. There were always so many rules, most of them unnecessary. I noticed a cricket and scooped it out. I looked around—there were a bunch of them. I scooped out another and another but they seemed to be multiplying, or else launching themselves right back in. I scooped out a fourth one and waited to see what it would do—it watched me watch it, still and patient.

I swam over to the ladder and climbed out.

On the way out, I said goodbye to Gabe, who was laughing and drinking with his friends as if he'd never met me.

————

Almost to our room, I hit my head on the low branch of a tree. The boys were still laughing—not at me, they hadn't seen me— but I felt it in my throat, my chest. Boys would always laugh at me. They'd never want me.

Elise parted my hair to take a look. "You're fine," she said.

She opened the door, and we immediately peeled off our swimsuits and soaked them in the sink like our mother taught us. I put on a clean pair of panties and a tank top, left a pair of shorts on top of my bag. Elise sat on her bed and cleaned out her purse; it was full of trash: wrappers and receipts, a pebble she launched across the room.

"Do you want anything from the vending machine?" she asked.

"A Kit Kat," I said, "And some Lay's—no barbeque."

"I'll be right back," she said, closing the door behind her.

I drank a mug of water and then another. I'd be up all night peeing. I was always doing stuff that I immediately regretted. I checked my head in the mirror but couldn't see anything. When

I pressed, though, I could feel my pulse, a strange alien thing. Then I backed up until I had a view of my body. If I kept my legs slightly apart, there was a tiny triangle of light that peeked through. I wanted to starve myself until the space grew larger and larger, until I was the skinniest, most beautiful girl in the world.

Elise came back with two bags of Lay's, a Kit Kat, and some Famous Amos cookies. We sat on her bed and ate everything, fast, and then I got in my own bed and watched her brush her hair. She could have been in a hair commercial, trying to convince me that Suave or some other cheap shampoo was responsible. I hated those commercials; there was no shampoo in the world that could make my hair look like that.

When she was finished, she picked up the remote and changed the channels until she came to a documentary on the Appalachian Trail, the camera panning over the mountains. It was over 2,100 miles long and went from Georgia all the way to Maine. From above, it looked treacherous, just a little path running over the mountains. We decided that one day we'd hike it together. We'd hike the entire thing, and we'd have trail names that started with "Moon" and "Rain," like the girls in the documentary.

"I smoked too much," Elise said. "My heart's beating so fast."

"You should stop smoking."

"Maybe I will, but not for the baby." She turned away from me and said, "I'm not going to ever be a mother. I'd be a terrible mother."

"You'd be a good mother," I said, but I didn't know if she'd be a good mother or not. She liked to go to parties and drive around with her friends.

———————

When Elise was asleep, I got out of bed and put on my shorts as quietly as possible, took a key off the table, and slipped out.

All of the lights were on and the curtains were open in room 212. I wanted to be a curtains-open kind of person, a person who smiled at strangers on the street—not just dogs and babies but beautiful people, too. Sometimes I could be this type of person. I'd feel so good and happy and it was like I'd never felt any other way, but the next day I'd be afraid again.

Charlie saw me and opened the door before I could knock.

Their room was exactly like ours except backward, the same dull landscape pictures on the wall.

"Hey, girl," Gabe said. He scooted over and I sat next to him in bed. He handed me his beer.

"Your sister asleep?" Erik asked.

"Yeah."

"She didn't like us much," Charlie said.

"Not really," I said.

I knew it was coming and then Erik said she was a knockout and I agreed. My heart was beating fast. I moved a hand to my neck and tried to make it seem like I wasn't checking my pulse.

The door opened and four people came in—three girls and a guy. Gabe stood and led me to the bathroom. "You aren't going to like these people," he said, locking us in. "The girls are loud and everybody gets so fucked up they puke and shit themselves."

He sat on the edge of the tub and I pressed my back to the door and slid down.

"They shit themselves?"

"Sometimes, but mostly they just puke." He dropped the toilet lid and said it was our table. "We've got everything we need here—beer, a toilet, drinking water. I think we could be very happy." He smiled. He was a lot better-looking when he didn't smile but it was nice to be smiled at. And you couldn't tell someone not to smile. It would be like saying, *Don't be happy. I don't like it when you're happy.*

"I hit my head earlier. Do you see a bump?"

He lowered himself to the floor and parted my hair, searched my scalp. "I don't see anything," he said, putting his hands above my knees.

"I'm a good girl."

His hand moved to my thigh. "I know."

"I don't even date."

"That's because you're a fundamentalist," he said, squeezing.

I thought about telling him I'd spent my whole life believing everything everyone had ever told me, but I didn't want him to think I was stupid. And I was changing all of that—I was going to start becoming my own person, figuring out who I was and what I believed in.

"I like this t-shirt," I said, rubbing the thin cotton between my fingers. It had a picture of Jeff Bridges on it.

"The muse of the age," he said, examining the ring on my necklace. He slipped it on up to his knuckle.

"It's a purity ring."

"Your parents give it to you?"

"My dad. Elise and I both have them. We took pledges to stay virgins until marriage but they don't work."

"They don't work, huh?"

"No," I said, shaking my head. "Elise is pregnant."

"Shit," he said. "Damn."

"I know."

"I'm sorry," he said, and the problem didn't feel like it belonged to me at all after that. It was just a story I could tell him. I told him about the ball where we'd pledged our virginity, how it was held in a school gymnasium, my father on one knee. All the white flowers and white balloons, grape juice for toasting.

"I didn't know things like that existed," he said.

"Some black family in the country organized it. They had four daughters. One of them was like seven."

He touched my face and I closed my eyes and tried to concentrate—I had to enjoy it. I had to be fully in the moment so I could remember it forever. And then his hand was on my thigh again and my own hand moved instinctively to my other thigh, trying to feel what he felt. I put my face in his neck. He didn't smell like soap or cologne or food or alcohol or cigarettes or plants. He didn't smell like earth or salt or pickles or rain or honey or anything I could name. I wanted to be able to name it. How could I remember if I couldn't name it?

"We just met but I feel like I know you," I said. I'd always wanted to say that to someone. It wasn't true but it wasn't not true, either. There was something about him that I recognized.

"You're easy to talk to," he said, leaning forward. "And I like the way you look at me."

"How do I look at you?"

"Like that," he said.

"I'm sure lots of girls look at you like this," I said. I was attempting to look sexy by copying what I'd seen on TV—a combination of sleepy and hungry. He leaned forward and I turned my head. I wasn't ready for him to kiss me yet. "What are y'all doing in a motel room if you live here?" I asked.

He reached behind him and turned on the shower. "We just stay here sometimes."

"How come?"

"Because we can do whatever we want and no one bothers us."

"Do you tell your mom you're spending the night with Erik and Erik tells his mom he's spending the night with you or something?" I asked.

"My mom doesn't care. If she wants to find me, she'll call, but she usually doesn't. I'm trying to create some ambiance," he said. "What do you think? Is it putting you in the mood?"

"It sounds like a shower," I said.

"We could take one together."

"I don't think so."

Outside, more people were arriving. There were many different voices now, but one loud girl stood out. We drank our beers and listened; I liked being hidden away with him, separate from the others. "How old are you?" I asked.

"Seventeen. How old are you?"

"Fifteen. Elise is seventeen."

"You seem older," he said, staring into my eyes.

I gathered my courage and held his gaze. It felt incredible. There were starbursts in the center of his eyes, little rods of yellow and green shooting out from the pupil like a doll's. But then there was a knock—it was the loud girl, saying his name.

"We're busy," Gabe said.

"I gotta take a piss," a guy said.

"Me too," said the girl.

"Piss outside."

"Fuck you, dude," the guy said.

"I can't piss outside," said the girl, and we sat there quietly until they went away.

"There's not much privacy here," he said, touching my hair.

"I'm not going to have sex with you," I said.

"I know," he said but his face changed briefly, like he hadn't known. He ducked out of the bathroom and grabbed a couple of beers from the sink, shut and locked the door behind him.

"I like you," I said when he was settled back onto the floor. "Why do you have to be all the way out in West Texas?"

"I like it out in West Texas," he said. "But then I've never really been anywhere else. What's Alabama like?"

"I don't know," I said, "it's different. The birds sound different. It's full of deer and paper mills and fat people. That makes it sound really bad, though—Montgomery's not that bad—I just wouldn't want to live anywhere else in Alabama. Except maybe Birmingham. Birmingham's okay, I guess."

"Are there Rebel Flags everywhere?"

"Sometimes, but it's good 'cause then you know who to avoid."

There was another knock and a different girl's voice—she sounded nice, said please. He stood and pulled me up.

"All right," he said. "Fuck."

"Thanks," the girl said. She was a pretty, bleached blonde with big brown eyes.

Three people were playing quarters at the table while Erik and a girl watched the muted TV. Outside, a group of people stood around, smoking cigarettes and talking.

"Hey," a guy said.

"I'm Jess," I said, sticking out my hand. He shook it, said it was nice to meet me. Gabe introduced me to the others. They were all attractive but still had one or two things wrong with them: acne, thick legs, kinky hair, moles that needed to be removed, hook noses, gums that showed too much when they smiled, eyes that were too far apart or close together. I didn't have to be perfect—hardly anyone was perfect. Why did I think I had to be perfect all the time? And all of these people were having sex. I looked around and thought, *You're having sex, and you, and you.*

Gabe said he had to get up at five and I wondered if I was boring him, or if there was some other girl that he wanted. Maybe the pretty, bleached blonde.

"Why do you have to get up so early?"

"I work construction with my dad," he said. "I'll probably sleep in my van for a few hours."

"It's still early," I said, though I didn't know what time it was—eleven o'clock, maybe later. I didn't want to go back to my room—there was nothing to do there but go to sleep and I didn't want to sleep. For once in my life, I felt like I was living and I wanted to stretch it out as long as I could.

"You could come with me," he said. "There's a bed in the back."

"You have a bed in your van?"

"It's my dad's van."

"That's kind of weird."

"But convenient," he said. "Wait here." He went back inside and grabbed a couple of beers, put a can in each pocket. Then we walked down the stairs and across the parking lot.

He opened the passenger-side door and I climbed in. It smelled like gasoline. I ducked into the back and sat on a mattress covered with a burnt-orange blanket. It was quiet for the few moments it took him to walk around and unlock his door, and I wondered what I was doing. I knew he wouldn't hurt me, but this was the kind of situation I had always been taught to avoid. It was risky behavior, how bad things happened. I thought of Acts 18:10: *"For I am with you, and no one is going to attack and harm you, because I have many people in this city."* I loved that—*"I have many people in this city."* The Bible could be so beautiful sometimes, if you could forget it was the Bible.

"It smells like gas," I said.

"I'll crack a window." He let the windows down halfway, and then he sat next to me and opened the beers.

"Is the van going to explode?"

"No," he said, laughing.

I told him I'd never done anything like this before, that I'd only kissed one boy in my life. I wanted him to know I wasn't the type to go off with a boy I'd just met even though it was exactly what I was doing and nothing I could say would change that. He stopped me by kissing me. His hands started to wander—they went under my shirt, the waistband of my shorts—and we started kissing more and more aggressively, and then I felt like I was with a stranger.

"Hold on," I said, pushing him back.

"What?"

"I want to see you." His pupils were larger now, and he seemed different, changed. "I can't see you," I said.

"Do you want me to turn on the light?"

"No—yes."

He stood and turned the light on, sat back down.

"Is that better?" he asked.

"Yes." He was the most perfect boy I'd ever seen. He tucked a piece of hair behind my ear and I took a long drink, finishing the can. I could feel the alcohol coursing through my veins and it felt good. It felt so good I thought about all of the beers I'd refused, all of the beers poured down the drain, behind bushes. I wanted them back. He touched my hair again and said it was soft and I set the can between my legs and leaned forward to kiss him. His hands stayed on my knees, my waist, places I wouldn't push them off.

"I liked you right away," I said, while he kissed my neck. "Right when I saw you."

"I liked you, too," he said.

"You weren't looking at my sister?"

"No."

"But she's so pretty."

"You're pretty, too," he said. "And you're fun and nice and I like the way you look at me."

"Really?"

"Really."

His face came at me, slowly, and he pressed his lips to mine. I tried to figure out how his mouth worked, his tongue. I wanted him to want me more than he'd ever wanted anyone. But then he pulled away and lit two cigarettes, handed me one. I held it between my fingers.

"I'll be right back," he said, getting to his feet. "Don't go anywhere." He opened the door and hopped out.

I climbed into the passenger seat and propped my feet on the dash, flicking ash before there was anything to flick. I imagined the van exploding, smoke and fire billowing into the sky. Gabe standing in front of room 212 screaming, and then running. I took another drag and dropped the cigarette out the window.

He returned with four beers and a joint. "Do you mind if I smoke this?" he asked.

"No," I said. "Do you mind if I don't?"

"Of course not."

We sat on the bed again and he lit the joint and inhaled. As soon as the last of the smoke left his mouth, I leaned forward and kissed him.

"How many people have you had sex with?" I asked.

"Why do all girls want to know that?"

"I don't know," I said. "You could always lie."

"I'm not going to lie."

"How many?"

"Seven," he said. "Is that a lot?"

I told him any number would seem like a lot to somebody who'd never done it. I wanted to know what the girls were like, if he'd loved any of them, but there wasn't enough time and he probably wouldn't tell me the truth, anyhow. I leaned forward to kiss him and he took my hand and brushed it against his shorts, the same swim trunks he'd had on earlier. I looked into his eyes as he pulled the string. He wasn't wearing anything underneath.

I touched him, letting him guide my hand up and down until I could do it myself. I watched his mouth, his closed eyelids, watched him pretend I could do something to him that no one else could.

———

Gabe walked me to my room, kissed me one last time.

"Will you think about me?" I asked.

"Of course," he said.

"And if the rapture comes and I'm not saved, you'll come for me?"

"Of course," he said again.

"Wait—how will you know?"

"You'll text me."

I told him I doubted cell phones would be working. He said

we'd figure it out and kissed me again. When he pulled away, I grabbed his hand.

"I have to go," he said. "I have to be at work in a few hours." He kissed my cheek and turned and I watched him walk away. He didn't look back. I wondered if he thought about looking back.

Elise didn't stir when I opened the door. I brushed my teeth and got into bed as quietly as I could.

"Did you have sex with him?" she asked, sounding wide awake.

"No."

"That's good."

"Why?" I said.

"No use in having sex with somebody you'll never see again. It would only hurt your feelings."

"I told him I wasn't going to," I said, holding up my hand in the dark. It had his cell phone number on it. I hoped it wouldn't smear or fade before I'd had a chance to transfer it to my phone.

"That's what all girls say before they do it," she said.

"Nuh-uh."

"I've said it and then gone ahead and done it," she said. "Sometimes it's just easier."

"That's sad."

"It's not that big a deal."

"It's a big deal to me," I said.

"That's because you haven't done it—most of the time it's like nothing. It's hard to believe something that's so much like nothing can mess you up so bad."

I thought about Gabe's dick in my hand, how he'd gasped as

he'd come and bit his lip. No one's ever done that to me before, he'd said, using only their hand.

"You're stronger than I am," Elise said. It was something she'd said before, something I hated, because she was so obviously stronger than I was. Even if there were ways in which I was stronger, they were small and nobody could see them. Elise asked for things and people gave them to her. She talked and they listened. I thought of all the people I'd met who hadn't even remembered me, people I'd had to introduce myself to again and again because I occupied so little space in the world.

"Good night," I said.

"Good night," she said. "I love you."

I brought my shirt to my nose and inhaled, breathing him in and out, in and out, until I could no longer smell anything.

FRIDAY

I awoke to a knock on the adjoining door, interrupting a good dream. It was right there, right where I could remember it if I tried, but there was another, more persistent knock, and I got out of bed.

My mother was standing there, eating a Fiber One bar. "We're leaving in fifteen minutes," she said, "your father wants to make it to California today."

"There's no way we can make it to California today," I said, though I didn't know if we could or not. She took another bite. I hated to watch her eat—she enjoyed herself too much and made a lot of noise. "I want one of those."

"It's the last one," she said. She pointed it at me and I took it and bit off a hunk. It was thick and chewy and seemed like too much trouble once I had it in my mouth.

She closed her door and I closed mine. She turned her lock so I turned mine.

I got back in bed and tried to remember my dream, but there was nothing, not an image or a feeling or anything. I listened to my parents' voices through the wall. It made me realize how infrequently they said more than a few words to each other, how they spoke mostly to convey information. I wanted someone I could tell everything to, someone who would spend a lot of time talking with me about nothing.

I went over to the window and looked out at the parking lot. Gabe's van was gone. He was hammering nails into a roof somewhere, or drinking black coffee like a grown man. I transferred his number to my phone and got in the shower. Something was wrong with the plumbing, the pipes making a high-pitched whine—up an octave and back down and then up again. The hot water went out and I stepped to the side to wait for it to return.

"I'm not wearing King Jesus today," Elise said when I came out.

"Who cares?"

"They'll care."

"I doubt they'll say anything," I said.

"Of course they'll say something, why wouldn't they say something?"

I sat on her bed and poked her through the spread. "They might have bigger fish to fry."

"What kind of fish?"

"They've been talking for half an hour," I said.

"They never talk."

"I know, that's what I'm saying."

We were quiet, listening, but one of them turned on the TV—probably our mother.

Elise went to the bathroom and I watched a movie I'd seen before, Brad Pitt playing one of the white trash characters he liked so much—too thin with a dirty beard, dirty hair, and dirty clothes, but he still didn't look trashy. I turned it off and knelt beside the bed. "*Hello, God. It's me.*" I couldn't think of anything to say after that and then I started wondering if everyone said *it's me*. To be *me* for someone, you had to be close to them—not their number one, perhaps, number one could just start talking, but close enough. Was it an attempt to feel closer to Him, claiming to be *me*? I squeezed my eyes shut. "*I haven't been very good. I've had a lot of doubts.*" I opened my eyes and stared at the ceiling, tried to look pained. He could see through all of it. "*I'm not sure I believe in you anymore. I'm not sure if I'm talking to myself, if I've always just been talking to myself.*" *Birds chirping*, I thought. Nothing. But then I was thinking about the rapture and being lifted into the clouds with all of the other chosen ones. I didn't want to die on earth or up in the clouds. I wanted God, if He did exist, to stay where He was, just like He always had. And I wanted my life to be different and better, but I wanted to be the one responsible for changing it.

I kept thinking, confusing myself, and then I stopped and listed all of the things I was sorry for—weakness of character, rebelliousness, being disrespectful to my parents, touching Gabe and letting him touch me. Wanting to be loved too much. But my desires weren't that unreasonable, and why was my body made to want things it shouldn't want? And then I had to start over, asking forgiveness and trying my best to want what I was seeking.

Elise came out of the bathroom. "What are you doing down there?" she asked.

"What's it look like?"

She shook her head.

"I can pray if I want," I said.

"Of course you can—pray away. Say one for me, too." She struggled to open a package of single-serve coffee. Once she got the little plastic container out, she had trouble sliding it into the slot, and it hit me—she would never amount to anything. But this wasn't true. She was smart and beautiful and people loved her. She would be a star. I would always be watching her.

———

I began to sweat the moment I stepped outside. I glanced over at Gabe's room and imagined his friends asleep, sprawled out on the floor. His van was still gone. One day it would be back but I wouldn't be around to see it.

We put our bags and suitcases in the trunk and our father got back on I-10. We didn't say anything about the real America—we preferred the interstate, where there were gas stations at more regular intervals and we didn't expect to see anything of interest. As soon as he started driving, though, I was reminded that it didn't matter whether we were on the interstate or the highway; the towns were small and far apart and there wasn't anything between them.

I checked to see how much gas we had: less than a quarter of a tank.

"What are you doing?" my father asked. "Put your seatbelt on."

"Seeing how much gas we have."

"We have plenty."

Driving was boring. Everything was boring. It was hard to believe that so much money had been spent to build roads where so few people traveled.

"What's the caravan up to?" I asked.

"I don't know," Elise said, opening a magazine.

At the next town, our father stopped at one of the gas station/houses, a single car at the pump. He parked on the other side and I looked over at the man, banging on the inside hood of his car with a hammer. Our father only liked to stop at Shell stations and Texacos—big, overly lit places with too many cars in the lot—so this had to be stressing him out. He got out and the man stopped banging.

"It's like straight out of a horror movie," Elise said.

"We're not having enough fun for this to be a horror movie," I said.

"You're right—we'd need a Jeep and some loud music and a couple of douche-baggy guys. And you'd have to be hotter."

"Don't be mean."

"I'm *kidding*," she said. "You're plenty hot. We'd just need to put you in something trashy, and a pair of Spanx."

"Y'all need to be nice to each other," our mother said.

"We're all we've got," Elise said.

Whenever we fought, our mother reminded us that one day they'd be dead and it would just be the two of us. It made me wish they'd had more children.

Our father came back and handed me a key. We took turns using the bathroom, which was nicer than I'd expected. There was even a candle on the toilet.

Inside the store, I selected a package of strawberry coconut cakes. I liked them because they were so pink and round. I took them up to the counter where Elise and my mother were waiting with an assortment of snacks and drinks.

"You live out here all by yourself?" Elise asked the guy behind the counter. He was clean and neat, normal-seeming. Our mother took out her wallet and moved my sister aside.

"Uh-huh," the man said.

"What do you do out here?" she asked.

"Work, hunt, fish," he said without looking at her.

"Do you hunt turkey?" she asked. He nodded. "Quail?" He nodded. "Dove?" He nodded. "Pigeon?"

"No pigeon," he said, scrunching up his face. He handed our mother the bag and walked to the back of the store.

"Where's your shirt?" our father asked Elise when we were back in the car.

"It smelled bad," she said.

"Your mother just washed them."

"That was the day before and it's like a hundred and eight degrees," she said, adding that cleanliness was next to Godliness.

"Well, enjoy your day off," he said, reminding her that he had paid twenty dollars for them.

"Each," I said, digging my cakes out of the bag. I opened the plastic, slid the tray out.

"Let's talk," Elise said.

"Oh, now you want to talk. I'm sorry. I'm busy."

"You're not busy."

"I don't like to talk about the stuff you like to talk about."

"What do I like to talk about?"

"Politics and stuff."

"I wasn't going to talk about politics," she said. "Forget it." She put her earbuds in. I looked at my cakes and thought of Gabe. Would he like me more if I was skinnier? I wanted him to touch me and feel bones beneath my skin. Boys liked it when you were starving, like you had starved yourself for them.

————

Our father hit something and a tire blew—flopping and bumping as he directed the car onto the shoulder. We got out and walked around it, the front passenger's side tire nearly gone. Our mother took the manual out of the glove box and handed it to our father. Then she went to the trunk and took bottles of water out of the cooler, passed them around. I had to pee but I twisted off a cap and took a drink.

"Do we have Triple A?" Elise asked.

"It expired two months ago," our mother said, placing the back of her hand on her forehead like she was taking her temperature.

"We don't need Triple A," our father said. He shielded his eyes and looked into the distance. Then he went to the trunk and started pulling things out, laying them on the pavement one by one like he had never seen any of it before. "Come on over here and help me," he said.

"I have to use the bathroom," I said.

"You have the worst bladder," Elise said. "You have to pee every hour."

"I drink a lot of liquids."

"Go find a tree," my mother said. In the sun, I could see just how thin her hair had gotten, how much of her scalp shone through.

"Worst. Bladder. Ever," Elise said.

I looked around—there weren't any trees—and then I realized that this was why the sky was so much bigger in Texas. In Alabama, pine trees lined the roads, skinny sickly pines pressed close together.

The few scrub bushes were pretty far away. I started walking toward them. The grass grew taller and taller and I thought about snakes, coiled and hissing, ready to strike. I wondered whether I could make bad stuff happen by imagining it. I knew at any moment I'd see a snake and it would bite me and I'd yell really loud and everyone would come running. It would be poisonous, of course, and they'd tell me I was going to be fine, that help was on its way, and I'd make them promise a million times and I'd believe them and then I'd die before I knew what was happening.

I stopped short of the bushes and squatted. *Nothing lasts forever,* I thought. *But I'm here now. I am here right now and I am peeing in a field*. I could have peed for longer but I jiggled and pulled up my shorts and began walking back, lifting my feet high and continuing the search for snakes.

"I have to go, too," Elise said, "but I'm gonna hold it."

I sat next to her on the side of the road and watched her tie her shirt into a knot so her stomach showed. My father didn't ask me to help him. He was still arranging his tools on the pavement and had already managed to rip his pants even though he hadn't done anything. I started thinking about his faults, which were many, and which he seemed totally unaware of. I wondered what my faults were, what people thought they were.

"Aren't you getting gravel in your hands?" I asked.

"No," she said. "You just worry about yourself."

"Fine, be a bitch."

"They're slowing down," Elise said, as a white pickup truck pulled onto the shoulder. "And they're stopping. Now they're getting out."

I looked around—there were no other cars in sight.

Three men got out of the truck, an older man and two younger ones. The older man smiled the kind of smile that's meant to make you feel comfortable, so it doesn't. He was tall and clean-shaven, wearing jeans and cowboy boots. I was afraid but reminded myself that I'd be afraid of any men that pulled over to help us, so my fear wasn't an indicator of anything. My fear was all out of whack because I was always afraid. My mother said I'd been an easy child: a quick delivery, I'd practically fallen out. I'd slept well and held out my arms to strangers, had begun to potty train myself at eleven months. I didn't remember this easy child. Surely this was my truest self, this person I had been in the beginning.

"Y'all got some car trouble?" the older man asked. His belt buckle was a real, actual snake's head. I elbowed Elise and she untied her shirt.

"It's a snake," I said.

"What is?"

"His belt buckle."

"We had a blowout," our father said, walking toward them with his hand outstretched.

"No problem," the man said. "We got it."

Our father protested mildly before thanking them and moving off to the side. He stood next to our mother and we were lined up like the characters in a Flannery O'Connor story I'd read in school. "The grandmother didn't want to go to Florida." That was the only line I remembered. "The grandmother didn't want to go to Florida." I didn't know what it was about that sentence that stood out to me, why I remembered it.

As the men worked, Elise and I shared earbuds, listening to the same songs as beads of sweat welled up from improbable places on my body. Sweat ran down my sides, trickled down my legs and arms.

"I like this," I said. "Who is it?"

"Katy Perry. You don't know who Katy Perry is?"

"Yeah, I know her."

"Name another song," she said, staring at one of the younger guys. She scratched her shoulder and touched her hair, trying to get his attention.

The older man let out a hacking cough and I jumped, my heart speeding up; any unexpected noise could startle me. My mother said it was because I read Stephen King novels before bed. She always had simple explanations like this, which made it hard for me to consider her advice. My favorite was *Duma Key*. I also liked *It* and *The Tommyknockers*. The books frightened me but it didn't make me not want to read them. This seemed to imply something defective in my character. It was like the other things I did to make my life harder—eating too much when I knew I'd get a stomachache, drinking water when I had to pee and there was nowhere to use the bathroom.

The men moved fast, like they'd done this a hundred times, but then there was some problem getting the donut on and they stood around looking at it, forming a tight little circle so we couldn't see what was going on. It wouldn't take much for them to steal our money and our car, to kill us. Or they could simply change our tire and get us back on the road, our faith in humanity restored. Both options seemed equally likely. I imagined them discussing how it was going to go down, which one of them would make the transition from nice guy to killer.

Elise pinched my leg, and my mother and father, standing above us, waited for the judgment. I imagined them asking us to turn around. Elise and I would stand, slowly, so slowly, and my father would take my hand and then we would all take each other's hands. We would remember in this moment how much we loved one another, how we would do anything to spare even one of us. But then the tire was in the trunk and the spare was on and my mother was offering them bottles of water. My father took out his wallet and tried to give them forty dollars, which they refused.

"This spare's about had it," the older man said, kicking it with his boot. "Where you headed?"

"Oakland," my father said.

"You've got a long way to go."

"We're on a pilgrimage," I said. "For the rapture."

The men continued to stand there, nodding and smiling with their hands in their pockets.

"The end times?" I said.

The one who was supposed to pull out a gun or a knife was hesitant now, unwilling. I smiled above them, into the sun. I was good. I was a good girl.

"All right," one of the young ones said.

"Y'all be safe," said the other.

When they pulled onto the road with a wave, Elise and I stood and brushed ourselves off.

————

We got in our car and sat there, letting them put distance between us. I ran my fingernail back and forth against the seat, making a nice little pattern like a freshly mown lawn.

"Is everything okay?" my mother asked.

"It's fine," my father said, agitated. He pulled onto the road, but he wouldn't drive over fifty and kept talking about where we were going to get a tire. There weren't any tire stores out here; there wasn't anything out here. As if to help him, I dutifully watched out the window for signs of life. The interstate markers ticked by and the signs preceding each exit let us know there was no reason to stop. Sometimes the signs were completely blank except for the words "gas" or "food."

I got out my phone and typed Gabe a message. I erased it and tried again. Nothing said what I wanted to say. Everything sounded generic, boring. I might as well have used the prewritten messages. I put my phone away and listened to my *Heaven* mix: "Tears in Heaven," "Knockin' on Heaven's Door," "Stairway to Heaven," "Heaven Is a Place on Earth." I'd made the mistake of limiting myself to songs with the word "Heaven" in the title whereas Elise had just gone with theme.

"What are you listening to?" Elise asked.

"Belinda Carlisle."

"Man, your mix sucks."

"Let's trade," I said, offering her my hot pink iPod. I'd regretted choosing pink the moment I'd stepped out of the Apple store.

"I'm listening to the Dalai Lama right now," she said, and leaned her head against the window, closed her eyes.

I found a comfortable position and closed my eyes, too. I thought about my job—at least I wasn't at work. I already wanted to quit even though I'd only been there a month and a half. I had to haul huge blocks of ice from the freezer in the back of the store to the machine at least six times a day. The rest of the time, I stood at the window, taking orders and making snow cones for bratty kids and their young mothers. I didn't like those mothers, how they assumed doors would be held for them and everyone would get out of their way because they had small children. I liked the boy who worked there, though, watching him change lightbulbs and move boxes around, and I liked the lady with the fake blue contacts who melted Nestlé's and poured it into molds. Her irises were an unnatural shade and there was a ring of dark brown around her pupils that made her seem alien.

After a while, my thoughts stopped making sense, but instead of slipping into sleep, I realized my thoughts were no longer making sense and I got so excited I was about to fall asleep that I jarred myself awake.

When I looked out the window again, there were more cars. Two lanes split into three and then four and then more lanes than I'd ever seen. I touched Elise but she was asleep, or pretending to sleep, so I left her alone. It was good to see cars again, good to see Starbucks and Taco Bells and gas stations that people didn't live in. A mountain range loomed in the distance, growing closer by the second, and the sky was clear except for some thin clouds like the streaks left behind by an airplane.

"Where are we?" I asked.

"El Paso, and Ciudad Juárez is right there to your left," my father said. "Surely this place is full of tire stores."

"Look, kids, it's a shantytown," Elise said, sitting up. She Googled Ciudad Juárez on her phone, and after the general Wikipedia entry, the first thing that came up was "Female homicides in Ciudad Juárez." She started reading it aloud, and I covered my ears because I didn't want to hear about women who were sold into slavery and killed at bus stops. Our cousin was murdered by a man who was never found, who would never *be* found. She was a drug addict and probably a prostitute and no one had bothered to find her killer. It wasn't like the TV shows, where detectives worked forty-eight hours straight and became close with the victims' families. I was sure it was the same with these women: they were poor; they shouldn't have been out at three o'clock in the morning. They were expendable. People were always saying the world was small but that was only to make it seem less terrifying. The world was so big. I hadn't realized how big it was until now.

My father got off at an exit and drove along the frontage road. Soon enough, we saw a tire store, the kind of place you don't see unless you're looking for it. He parked and we went inside and sat in a glassed-in waiting room with a TV in one corner, outdated magazines, and free coffee. It was like every other carwash and car-repair waiting room in the world, and I thought of all the Saturday mornings I'd spent with my father at Personal Touch. He'd read the newspaper while I watched the men clean and vacuum our car and then we'd go to Krispy Kreme, where I'd get my own bag of doughnut holes. I never thought about calories or fat grams then. I just ate and enjoyed eating and didn't get on the scale to watch my weight creep up.

It took less than half an hour for the old tire to come off and a new one to be put on, and we were back on the road, my father flying through El Paso, gunning it on the curves. He had once dreamed of being a racecar driver. He'd told me this one night when it was just the two of us having dinner, a rare moment when I'd responded to his questions with answers and he'd rewarded me by telling me something about himself. But it was probably just one of those dreams kids have, like they want to be an astronaut or a garbageman, the kind of thing no one actually wants to be when they grow up.

The downtown skyline was impressive—lots of tall buildings and a mountain backdrop. It was like the Old West, despite how big and concrete everything was. There was something about it that made it feel a million years old.

Soon we were in New Mexico, a state none of us had been to before. Our mother said she'd heard New Mexico had nice rugs; she wouldn't mind bringing home a nice rug.

"We don't need a rug where we're going," our father said.

"Then I don't see what the problem is with getting one," she said, which didn't make sense, but I knew what she was saying. Buy a rug or don't. Drive across the country or stay home. None of it really mattered.

"Anybody hungry?" he asked. "We've got choices here, we should probably take them." He pulled off at an exit and we were faced with the usual selection of fast-food restaurants.

"Burger King," Elise said.

"Taco Bell," I said.

Our mother also voted for Taco Bell. She liked the regular, crunchy-shell tacos, the kind of thing nobody ordered unless they were getting a dozen in a box. Our father agreed to go through the drive-thrus at both if we ate in the car. I didn't like to eat in the car because he might wreck and kill us all, but I didn't want Burger King, either. The only thing I really liked there was the chicken sandwich, and it was good, but I could get more at Taco Bell without looking like a pig.

I ordered some onion rings at Burger King, seven in the box, and a bean burrito, a chicken quesadilla, and a Frutista Freeze at Taco Bell.

"Let me have a sip of that," Elise said, and I passed my drink to her—strawberry on top and mango on bottom.

"You know this probably has like five hundred calories in it," she said, stirring it, messing the flavors up.

"Leave me alone," I said.

Our father pulled into a parking space and bowed his head. He said the standard prayer followed by a long-winded, rambling one in which he asked for guidance and courage. *You're going to need it*, I thought, popping an onion ring into my mouth and chewing quietly.

Elise slopped the condiments off her veggie burger with a napkin. She took a bite and said she thought it was MorningStar Farms. It hadn't occurred to her before but she was pretty sure it was MorningStar, the regular veggie patty, cooked to within an inch of its life. My mother unwrapped my father's double cheeseburger and secured a napkin around it, and he ate while reaching his other hand into the bag for fries. He steered with his elbows and knees, and when the car began to veer off the road, she reached over and took the wheel. I wondered what she thought of him now, if she still saw him as the man she'd married or if he was so different he was like a stranger. She'd told me once that she'd married him because he was ambitious and honest, which weren't qualities I'd have used to describe him at all. He had been handsome once, though, tall and slim with a full head of hair. Sometimes I got out their wedding album and flipped through the pictures. There was one in particular I liked: the two of them about to leave for their honeymoon. They stood in front of my father's sports car, and my mother wore an outfit she had bought special for the occasion, had had her hair and makeup done. They were about to fly to Hawaii, first-class. I knew my mother's suitcase had been lost, but the airline had given her the money to buy a whole new wardrobe, which she'd spent on beach hats, strappy sandals, and overly revealing dresses that she'd probably never worn again. My father hated to fly, and I couldn't imagine him agreeing to take her somewhere so far-off and exotic. I couldn't imagine them snorkeling and exploring the beaches, driving around in a rented jeep with the top down. It made me love them more because I knew the day would come when I would also be unrecognizable to myself.

New Mexico was going by quickly, dull and flat but otherworldly. There were strange flat shrubs and bunches of small trees I'd never seen before. In the distance, mountains loomed low and jagged. The Jesus billboards had been replaced by billboards telling us not to drink and drive, which our father said was due to all of the Indians. Their bodies didn't process sugar like ours did, so they were more susceptible to diabetes and alcoholism.

"You have diabetes," Elise said. "And they're called Native Americans, not Indians. Indians are from India."

Our father said he'd never met an Indian *or* a Native American that he liked.

"Hey," Elise said, and we looked out her window at some dust kicking up.

"Thrilling," I said, but I kept watching it and it *was* pretty mesmerizing, the way it moved. I'd never seen dirt act so purposefully. I fingered a tiny scrape on my knee from the bottom of the pool—reassurance that I hadn't dreamed Gabe. I thought about how he'd looked at me, the things he'd said. I thought about his body and his face and the smell of gas in his van. I was going to replay our time together so often I'd have it memorized forever. I was going to replay it so many times I'd never remember any new details.

After that we watched YouTube videos of people driving on I-10 in New Mexico, same as us; most of the videos were shot by a guy who went around the country filming sections of interstate. He'd added various facts and notes at the bottom—when certain projects would be completed, crime rates, the longest and tallest and biggest. The videos were strangely riveting. The speed was doubled or tripled and fast music played. When we ran out of interstate videos, we watched others: kids recording a dust storm they called a white devil, a couple in a motorhome driving across the country. The man kept saying things like "Confidence is high" in a cheerful voice while the woman talked to the dog in her lap. Elise and I speculated about the nature of their troubles, but her phone died and she had to pass it up front to charge it.

In Arizona, everything looked different again. I felt like all of the people who were always talking about the homogenization of America were wrong—each place really *was* different. There were McDonald's and Targets, but every town was full of different-looking people who had different accents and manners. In some places, the people said "Good morning" and "It's nice to see you," as if it wouldn't be the first and last time they'd be seeing you, but twenty minutes down the road, the people might be cow-faced and unfriendly.

We were charmed by the cactuses, like giant hands reaching into the sky, and the camel at the dollar store where we stopped to buy Pepto-Bismol and toothpaste.

While our parents went inside, Elise and I stood in the parking lot watching a man give camel rides on the little stretch of dirt. I'd never seen a camel before. It was ugly and the humps were closer together than I'd imagined. A young girl, wedged between them, held up a hand and her mother took a picture. Elise took a picture of her mother taking a picture. And then Elise took a picture of me standing in front of the camel with my own hand raised, squinting below the enormously blue and cloudless sky.

————

We didn't make it to California. At two o'clock, our father stopped at a casino resort somewhere near Phoenix. He pulled the car into the circular drive and waved the valet driver off.

"Why are we stopping?" I asked. "It's early."

"I'm going to check the rates," he said, getting out and taking the keys with him. There was a bounce in his step I hadn't seen in days. We were quiet as we watched him walk through the door.

"This place looks nice," I said.

"If you're into big, generic casino resorts," Elise said. "Which I am, don't get me wrong. They're a heck of a lot better than the places we've been staying."

"What's the deal?" I asked.

"The deal with what?" our mother said.

"She means last night we stayed at a ghetto motel and now we're at this luxury resort," Elise said.

"No, I mean why are we stopping so early. I thought he wanted to make it to California."

"He wants to gamble," Elise said. "He's desperate to get his hands on a slot machine."

"He's not going to gamble," our mother said, though we all knew he'd step onto the casino floor and the lights and sounds would trigger something in his brain, and he'd sit for hours, slipping twenty-dollar bills into machines. For years, he'd been sneaking off to the Indian casino on Eddie Tullis Drive, a beige monstrosity that could have doubled as a medical clinic.

"He gambles all the time," Elise said. "Everybody knows he gambles."

"Everybody does *not* know," our mother said. "I haven't told anyone, and you shouldn't either. It's nobody's business."

"We're not like you," Elise said. "We don't want to live like that."

"Like what?"

"Lying—pretending we've got money when we don't, that we're these perfect Christians who never do anything wrong."

"It's not lying."

"It's deception," Elise said.

"It's our reputation," our mother said.

"I don't care about my reputation."

"And it shows," our mother said, which was possibly the meanest thing I'd ever heard her say to my sister.

Elise paused dramatically and said, "I'm sorry I'm not the daughter you wanted."

I picked up an empty popcorn bag and stuffed candy and gum wrappers into it, passed it up. My mother took it and held it. It would be no fun being a mother, everybody handing you their garbage and wanting things all the time, nobody to tell your problems to. She could never say anything bad about our family. She could only talk about other peoples' problems as a way of talking about her own.

"I'm sorry you feel that way," my mother said. "It isn't true."

Elise was clutching her stomach. It occurred to me that I had no idea when the baby had been conceived; she could be a couple of weeks pregnant or several months. She might even be far enough along that she couldn't have an abortion, and then what would we do? I imagined taking her to a clinic set up in somebody's house, a woman bustling her inside before closing the door in my face, which was something I'd seen in a documentary. I didn't know anything except what I'd seen on TV and I never retained the information I learned. When I watched those outdoor programs, I didn't actually consider that one day I might be lost in the wild and need that stuff in order to survive. I thought about it, trying to recall something, and remembered the fat hippie saying I shouldn't eat brightly colored things, that brightly colored things are usually poisonous. If I was ever hungry and found a neon green insect under a log, I wouldn't make the mistake of eating it.

Our father got back in the car. "I got y'all your own room," he said, handing us key cards. "Might as well enjoy ourselves on our last night."

"That's what the 9/11 hijackers thought," Elise said. "They drank and got lap dances and then left a copy of the Qur'an on the bar."

"I hope you'll be with us," our father said, buckling his seatbelt.

"I'll be with you."

"I sincerely hope."

He drove through a maze of empty lots and parked, but a sign said no overnight parking so he backed out and kept winding around. It reminded me of that scene in *National Lampoon's Vacation* when Chevy Chase and his family arrived at Walley-World. There wasn't a single car in the lot and they parked so far away and Chevy Chase kept saying "First ones here!"

———

In the hotel lobby, there was a water wall behind the check-in desk, the casino floor only steps away, dinging with bells and whistles. We walked past a coffee shop and an ice-cream parlor, stores selling dreamcatchers and turquoise jewelry, quilted bags in paisley prints. We passed a Mexican restaurant and a sundries shop. I thought I'd buy a postcard and mail it to Gabe—it occurred to me that I'd never bought a postcard before. I had never been far enough from home. You didn't send someone a postcard from an adjoining state.

A man held the elevator and we got on. His wife was with him but he stared openly at Elise, and for the first time ever I was glad to be the unattractive sister. Who wanted to be stared at by ugly old men all the time? I wanted to kill him for her, wanted to kill all of them so she could live in peace.

Our parents got off at the sixth floor, followed by the man and his wife.

"We're in 610," our mother said, and the doors closed.

"Mom's as miserable as we are," I said, though I wasn't feeling miserable at all. I was excited, nearly thrilled. We had our own room in a nice hotel. There was a pool and room service and I had enough money to buy a dreamcatcher if I wanted.

"Catholics don't go in for this kind of stuff."

"Uncle Albert does," I said.

"Uncle Albert doesn't count—if he wasn't building a doomsday bunker, he'd be investing all his money in the Iraqi dinar or some other scheme. Don't you remember when he tried to get Dad to invest in that black apartment complex?"

"No," I said. "When was that?"

"A couple of years ago. It was a falling-apart slum."

"Nobody tells me anything."

"Mom tells me all sorts of things I don't want to know," she said. "Consider yourself lucky."

"When?"

"At night after y'all go to sleep, we watch *The Young and the Restless* and she tells me everything. It's terrible."

"You should go to your room and read like I do."

We turned a corner and walked a ways and then turned another corner and I knew I was going to have trouble finding my way back to the elevator. A cleaning lady stuck her head out of a room and we exchanged hellos. She was foreign but her hello had been perfected. I checked her cart for soaps and shampoos, but all of the best stuff had been hidden away somewhere.

We came to our room just as a tiny, severe woman opened the door across from ours and deposited a room service tray outside. She looked at me without any expression whatsoever. Her face was tight and smooth; it reminded me of a stone.

"Good afternoon," I said. I liked saying "good morning" so much better.

She made a humph sound and closed her door.

"Real friendly around here," I said, loudly.

Elise slid her key in, opened the door. Our room smelled like carpet cleaner, something that might be called Mountain Fresh or Ocean Breeze. We stood there with our bags, looking at an enormous whirlpool tub next to the king-sized bed.

"What is *this*?" she said. She stepped into the tub with her shoes on while I went into the bathroom. There was a shower and two sinks and a little TV, everything cool and white. I wanted to feel my bare feet on the tiles.

I flushed and washed my hands, walked around checking everything out. I opened drawers and closets, peeled the spread off the bed. Above it, there was a painting of two empty chairs on a beach. The picture bothered me—I didn't like it when places pretended to be other places; if people had wanted to go to those other places, they would have gone to them. Why go to Las Vegas to be in Paris? If you wanted to go to Paris, go to Paris.

Elise stepped up and down like she was walking in some kind of muck. "Let's put on our suits and get in."

I opened the curtains. Our room faced a parking garage that gave off a ghostly blue light. "Check out this view."

"You know the creepiest sound ever? A man whistling in a parking garage," she said. "And they never whistle anything in particular, it's just this random no-song whistling. They do it to creep people out—they know it creeps everybody out."

I picked up the phone and called our parents. Our mother answered on the fourth ring. I asked if they had a whirlpool next to their bed, and she said that they did. I asked if they had a view of the parking garage and she said they had a view of the pool and then she said to come down to their room at six-thirty for supper and hung up.

Elise got in bed and tested out the pillows to see how high they were, if she was likely to get a crick. Then she went to the bathroom and peed with the door open.

"There's a TV in here!" she called. "It looks like it's from 1989."

"I saw it."

We didn't know anything about 1989 but we referenced it a lot. It represented all of the movies we loved. It represented a time when the captain of the football team might actually fall in love with the homely red-haired girl, when they could make us believe it. I got in bed and Elise continued to talk to me from the bathroom. *Maybe we wouldn't have to drive tomorrow and we could just stay here. And what if the rapture actually happened and we got to watch it on TV? Wouldn't that be kind of amazing? There were Aveda products! She loved Aveda products!* I got out of bed and turned on the water in the tub. The pressure was bad—it was going to take forever to fill up. I kept turning the knob but the water didn't come out any faster. We could go down to the pool for an hour and come back and it still wouldn't be filled.

"I'm going to get ice," she said, clutching the bucket to her stomach.

"Okay, Dad."

———

"Come here," Elise said, setting the bucket on the table.

"What?"

"Just come."

I followed her to a room catty-corner from ours where a fat lady was sprawled on a king-sized bed, her purple dress bunched up like a tablecloth between her legs. Against one wall, there were four cages stacked on top of each other with two birds in each. Some of the birds were white and some were a pale, lovely pink.

"Mourning doves," Elise said.

The woman sat up, excited to have visitors. "Hey, hon," she said. "Come on in, make yourself at home." She was truly massive, wonderfully enormous, but her face was oddly thin. "Have some cheese and fruit, if you want. We were just about to have a snack."

"How'd you get the birds up here?" Elise asked.

"I tip people," the woman said. "Whenever I go to hotels, I carry a lot of small bills. You give people a handful and they don't even care if they're all ones."

The toilet flushed and a man came out of the bathroom. He was fat but not enormous, just normal fat, with a patchy beard.

"That's my son, Luke," the woman said, lighting a cigarette. "Luke and I travel everywhere together, don't we?" She leaned over the bed and produced an ashtray, set it on her stomach. I couldn't take my eyes off of her. She was magnetic, strangely beautiful, and had long strawberry blond hair. I imagined her at the beauty salon, having it highlighted, talking to people and laughing like she was just as good as anybody.

Luke stood there watching us, scratching his beard. His feet were planted shoulder-width apart.

"There's a male and female in each," Elise said, squatting to look in the cages. I knelt next to her.

"Did you know that mourning doves are monogamous?" the woman asked, waving her cigarette around. "They mate for life."

"I love monogamous animals," Elise said.

Luke laughed and my sister turned to look at him, her ponytail flying. He had the kind of eyes that couldn't look at you straight on—they were always slightly to the left or right, as if you were standing next to yourself.

"How can you tell which are male and which are female?" I asked.

"You put two together and see if they try to kill each other," the woman said. "That's why I stack 'em like that—if the males even see each other, they go berserk. Beat their wings and puff out their chests."

Elise stood and said, "Thanks for letting us look at them."

"Let's let 'em fly around," the woman said.

"Maybe later?" my sister said. "We just got here and we have to unpack and stuff."

"I trained them in the bathroom and now I can let 'em fly wherever. Even if I leave the door open, they don't fly away. If I'm not feeling well, they land on my chest and look at me like, *Dodo, you okay in there, Dodo?* They're very intuitive animals."

"Maybe later," Elise said.

"We'll be here," the woman said. "We're not going anywhere, are we, Luke? We were just about to have a snack."

Elise thanked her about fourteen more times and we went back to our room. I remembered my horoscope from a few days ago, how I was supposed to be asking questions and I'd hardly asked anybody anything. I should have asked the woman why she chose birds, or about the mating process—did the male and female always like each other, or was it a matter of trial and error? Or I could have asked where they were from, where they were going. It seemed silly that we were all moving around the world for no other reason than we could—cars and planes and boats taking people from one location to another as if we weren't all going to die.

————

Elise stood at the desk and flipped open the binder.

"How come you didn't want to see them fly?" I asked.

"Because that guy was creeping me out," she said. "Wasn't he creeping you out?"

"Yeah."

"He was a fucking creep."

"Probably a parking garage whistler," I said.

She picked up the phone and ordered a veggie burger with onion rings, a Diet Coke, and a piece of apple pie. If she hadn't asked for the pie, I might have believed she'd actually spoken to someone. She never ate pie.

"You didn't order anything," I said.

"What I really want is a cheeseburger. Actually, I think it's the baby who wants a cheeseburger." She stood in front of the mirror and looked around to see if there was enough space to do her jumps. "I'm going to call room service for real in a minute. What're you having?"

"Ice cream," I said.

She did a herkie and then three more in quick succession; they seemed so effortless, so easy, it made me think I could do them.

"Have you ever noticed how skinny people get vanilla and fat people get chocolate? And *really* skinny people get strawberry. I should probably start ordering strawberry, then I'll be skinny."

"I don't think it works that way," she said.

"It would be a start," I said. "It would be something."

"And you're not fat, you're just a little plump."

"I don't want to be *plump*, that's an awful word, don't ever say that to me again." I put my bag on the bed and started going through it. I missed the rest of my stuff. I missed our house, my bed. If we were at home, Elise and I would be outside on the trampoline. She'd insist I do a back handspring and spot me, taking her hands away at the last minute so she could tell me I'd done it on my own. The baby would already be a bad dream and I'd never mention it again, even when we were old, even if I was really pissed off.

She dialed room service and ordered a veggie burger and fries. "Strawberry?" she asked.

"A hot fudge sundae and a Diet Coke."

"And two hot fudge sundaes and two Diet Cokes," she said. She hung up and climbed into bed, spread out in the middle.

"You know how you said you never feel anything in church?" I asked.

"Yeah."

"I've been thinking about that."

"And?"

"I don't feel anything, either," I said.

"What about when you were saved?"

I shook my head. "It never even occurred to me to think about whether I was feeling something, or if I believed or not. Do you think I'm stupid?"

"No," she said. "I think you're a kid."

"I want to believe," I said.

"I know you do."

"Maybe I should talk to Brother Jessie."

"Call him," she said. "I'm sure he'll talk to you."

I took the Bible into the bathroom and sat on the cool tile, opened it and read: " . . . *many will turn away from the faith and will betray and hate each other, and many false prophets will appear and deceive many people . . . the love of most will grow cold, but the one who stands firm to the end will be saved.*" Did standing firm mean believing in the rapture or not believing in it? Was Marshall a false prophet or a man trying to instill faith? Everything had become confusing all of a sudden. Was Elise betraying me or was I betraying her? I went back into the room and climbed in bed next to her, closed my eyes and opened the Bible to a random page.

"What are you doing?" she asked.

"'*Jesus said to him, The foxes have holes, and the birds of the sky have nests, but the son of man has nowhere to lay his head.*'"

Elise took the Bible, opened the drawer, and dropped it in. "We're not playing Bible 8-Ball right now," she said. She was watching the hotel's station, jazzy music and a smooth-talking man telling us about the hotel's amenities. We watched pretty women laugh with their mouths open wide, lightly touching the shoulders of their handsome men. We toured each of the restaurants—the Mexican cantina, the steakhouse, the burger stand, the Irish pub—before moving on to the casino floor. We learned how many slot machines there were, how many table games. Craps lessons were held every afternoon at two o'clock and the annual poker tournament was at the end of the month. We toured the hotel rooms and the pool with its outdoor bars, the gym and spa, and then we were back at the pretty laughing women. We watched it all the way through a second time.

After our third trip through the restaurants, I asked her how many times we were going to watch it.

"Forever," she said.

"How come you're not calling Dan? You're not even Googling anything."

"*Dan*? Who cares about Dan?"

"You do."

"It's not like I love him."

"Why would you date someone you didn't love?"

She looked at me like she couldn't believe I'd asked that. "You'll see," she said ominously.

"I'm not going to ever be with someone I don't love."

"You will," she said. "You won't believe the things you'll do." She handed me the remote control and got out of bed, picked up her suitcase. "When the food comes, just sign your name, the tip's already been added." She closed the door to the bathroom.

I changed the channels. On *Wheel of Fortune,* three nervous college students in their big college sweatshirts took turns spinning the wheel. As usual, they weren't attractive or charming and I wondered how they'd been selected. I hadn't watched it in a long time, but quickly remembered how all of the puzzles seemed so obvious once they were revealed, how stupid it made me feel.

At the bonus round, there was a knock. I opened the door

and the guy walked past me with a tray, asked where he should put it.

"The bed." He set it down and handed me the bill in a black book and I added another three dollars on top of all the tips and fees that had already been figured. He let himself out and I sat on the bed. I dug a spoon into my sundae, the ice cream still solid.

I muted the TV to listen for Elise, and then turned it to Anderson Cooper to try and lure her out.

"Anderson's talking about the Eurozone again," I called.

"Fuck the Eurozone," she called back.

A few minutes later, she came out of the bathroom with her hair in a towel and got in bed next to me. We ate our hot fudge sundaes and drank our Diet Cokes and then she cut her veggie burger in half and everything felt right and good.

———

Elise slingshotted a pair of yellow bikini bottoms at me. She had at least eight swimsuits, which I considered an excessive number, but when you were beautiful you could insist on needing more, requiring more, and people would provide.

She put on her white one, the ruffles on top to make her chest look bigger. She hardly ever wore the white one because she didn't want to get it dirty. She let her hair down and stood sideways in front of the mirror. There was a long pause while we assessed her stomach. She touched it, ran her hand over its smooth, flat surface. Her belly button was so deep you couldn't see the bottom of it, but it was going to turn inside out.

"Do you know how many weeks?" I asked.

"No," she said.

I took my swimsuit into the bathroom. It was still slightly damp; it felt awful, wedging it over my thighs.

We left all the lights and the TV on.

"Let's take the stairs," Elise said.

I didn't feel like it, but I followed her to the stairwell. It wasn't the kind that was meant for guests—concrete and gray, boxes of Urine Off advertising itself in neon yellow letters. We didn't see anyone, but there were room service carts with trays of old food and housekeeping carts with stacks of freshly laundered towels.

"I'm not taking the stairs back up," I said.

"You do what you want," she said, "and I'll do what I want."

On the first floor, there was a table set up in the hallway that blocked the entrance to the pool, two guys sitting at it. They said we needed wristbands to get into the pool area, told us to write our names and room number in their book. They were brusque and mustached and important.

"I forget our room number," Elise said. "Do you remember it?"

"No," I said.

"You don't know where you're staying?" the older security guard asked, chuckling.

"We're staying here," Elise said. "We just checked in." She found her room key in its little envelope and set it on the table and one of the guys wrote down the number. I held out my hand for the other guy to give me the wristband but he insisted on putting them on us. Then he stood and held the door.

"Jesus," Elise said. "It's like Fort-fucking-Knox."

There were a lot of people milling about—couples and groups of boys and multicultural families, pretty girls like Elise taking drink orders. Old people. Babies. It was good to see so many of them. We walked to the far side of the pool and took off our dresses. After looking around to see who was looking at me—no one—I got out my phone and called Shannon. She picked up, sounding like she always sounded, slightly hoarse like she was still in bed.

Shannon and I had a very one-sided relationship—I asked her questions and she told me how bad things were, how they would never change. At the end of every conversation, she'd realize she had talked the entire time and say something like *Next time we're going to talk about you,* though we never did, and I was mostly okay with it. Hearing her complain about her life made me feel better about my own—her life really *was* pretty shitty. But this time, when she asked how I was, I didn't say fine and ask about her stepmom or the boy she liked who didn't like her back. I told her about Gabe, relayed some of the sweeter things he'd said. I could tell she wasn't happy about it. She said she was happy but she sounded very down and tried to steer the conversation back to herself. I told her he wanted to see me again and was trying to figure out a way to make that happen, that we were maybe in love. She said I should be careful—she didn't want to see me get hurt.

"I'm not going to get hurt," I said.

"I hope not," she said. "I just know how excited you get."

I didn't like the way the conversation was going anymore.

She was making me feel bad and I was tired of feeling bad. I was tired of relying on her unhappiness to make myself feel better. I wanted new friends, fun girls who laughed a lot and liked to do new things and go new places. Shannon and I always went to the same café where we sat in the same booth and ate the same sandwiches and my life was never going to be any different that way.

"That's him on the other line now," I said.

"It is?"

"Yeah."

"You're so lucky," she said. "I wish I had a boy."

"I'll call you when I get home," I said, and hung up.

Elise raised her eyebrows but didn't say anything.

"You want to get in the pool?" I asked.

"Not right now, but Mom and Dad are over there if you want somebody to play with."

They were in their swimsuits, the same ones they'd been wearing for the past decade. My mother's was black with yellow flowers, so worn out it was nearly see-through. My father's was navy blue with white stripes down the sides. It was their day at the pool, but the one time we were at a decent place all bets were off.

"Tell me something from Cosmo," I said.

"Men like sex, no fatties," she said. "It's the same thing in every goddamn issue."

I'd never heard her say "*goddamn*" before. I was shocked. I wanted to hear her say it again. I adjusted my swimsuit and walked to the pool's edge, climbed onto the little shelf. Then I lowered myself in and breaststroked over to my parents. My mother was sitting on a step while my father stood in water up to his belly button. He was moving his arms around and looking about distractedly like people do when they're peeing. I sat next to my mother.

"Are you having fun?" she asked.

"Yeah," I said. "It's so nice here." They always wanted to know if I was having fun. It made me sorry I didn't have more fun.

"We're about to go up," she said. "We just came down for a minute to cool off."

My father patted my back as he stepped out and asked if I was having fun. I told him I was and took off, swimming in and out of groups of kids and boys, listening while trying to appear uninterested.

"Here she comes, she's coming this way," one of the guys said, on my third lap. I swam a wide arc around a couple of kids playing colored eggs to avoid them. "And there she goes," he said. Maybe I wasn't unattractive. If I moved to Arizona, I might be popular. I might be on the dance team, kicking my legs in tall boots at pep rallies. I hadn't made the dance team in Montgomery and didn't know if I was going to try again. It seemed better to accept the one failure than to try a second time and fail, like I hadn't learned my lesson.

I was wearing my cutest swimsuit, a black one-piece with ovals cut out of the sides, and a worn-in baseball cap that belonged to one of Elise's ex-boyfriends. She had a lot of ex-boyfriend stuff—t-shirts and ball caps and koozies—and she usually wouldn't say anything if I confiscated something until it was mine. I liked their t-shirts best, which were always thin and soft, tiny holes around the neck and waist. I didn't know what they did to get them that way.

I got out and resumed my place next to my sister.

"Let's order a drink," she said, raising the flag on the back of her chair. "They've already gone. I'm sure Dad's dying to get his hands on a slot machine. Raise the flag on your chair, too."

Almost immediately, a pretty pool girl came over and Elise ordered two piña coladas. She didn't ask to see our IDs. Elise signed her name and our room number and, a few minutes later, our drinks came in small white buckets: cold and sweet, I could hardly taste the liquor.

When they were empty, we put our flags back up. Elise signed our name and room number and fresh ones appeared like magic. The more I drank, the closer I looked at things—a beach ball spinning on the water, the pink and blue and yellow panels going round and round, a girl wading into the water with a cast on her arm, cocked at a ninety-degree angle. The dark spots in the clouds. Elise wouldn't stop reading her magazine, so I got back in the pool. I swam toward the group of boys while one of them stepped steadily backward until he was right in front of me. I stood in three feet of water and said hello. He was tan with strong arms and a stomach full of well-defined muscles. He was old but I couldn't tell how old because of the mirrored sunglasses and baseball cap.

He asked me a few questions and then I was in his arms, my neck thrown back so my hair dragged the water. My hat floated away and he fetched it and emptied the water out, set it back on my head.

"Is that your sister?" he asked, nodding at Elise.

"Yeah."

"Why don't you call her over?" he said, and I told him she'd come if she wanted to. I looked into his sunglasses, trying to see what he saw. There was only my face—my nose distortedly large, my hair slicked and smooth. I leaned back and he spun me in slow circles, first one way and then the other.

He started telling me about himself, how he'd started a website to help people find jobs, how it was becoming very successful. He was on a trip with friends and next they'd go to Las Vegas to play poker. I thought about the Las Vegas girl, wondered if they would encounter her somewhere, or pass her on the street.

I looked at Elise's chair but she wasn't in it. I found her talking to a lifeguard, a short boy with a red floaty slung over his shoulder.

"I'll be right back," I said, and swam over to her. "Come over here with me," I said, interrupting her conversation. The guy was kind of fat for a lifeguard. If he could pass the test, I might pass, too.

"In a sec," she said.

I swam back to the boys and Elise followed as the lifeguard climbed onto his perch.

We let them buy us a third drink and made plans to meet

later, plans that Elise said we'd break if anything better came along, but I couldn't imagine anything better coming along. The only thing that might be better than these boys were other boys.

———

At dinner, we sat at a circular table too big for the four of us. It made me feel lonely and far away from everything. I concentrated on the alcohol moving in and out of parts of my body I'd never felt before. When the dining room went quiet, there was a buzz in my ears like a lightbulb.

Though I'd hardly said a word, it seemed unlikely that my mother wouldn't know. I avoided her eyes. She would be angry and disappointed if she found out, and I didn't want her to look at me differently. If I wasn't the good daughter, I wouldn't know what I was. I wasn't popular or a cheerleader or a straight-A student. I wasn't on the dance team. I wasn't a member of the Student Council or even the Key Club. There were so many things I wasn't that I had difficulty defining myself, especially in relation to Elise, who was so many things.

My father ordered a bottle of red wine and asked the waiter for four glasses.

"John," my mother said. "These kids aren't drinking."

"It's a special occasion," he said. "Just for toasting."

"Absolutely not," she said.

The waiter came back with a bottle and poured an inch of wine in my father's glass, waited for him to take a sip.

"Taste it," Elise said, which he did, nodding pleasantly.

Then the waiter went around the table, pouring us each a quarter of a glass.

"We're about ready to order," my father said.

"I haven't even opened my menu yet," Elise said.

The waiter said he'd give us a few minutes and set the bottle down. Elise grabbed it and filled her glass. Then she filled mine, as well. My mother handed me hers and we swapped. When the dining room went quiet again, the buzz in my ears returned. It was oddly pleasant.

"We have a lot to celebrate," my father said. "Tomorrow we go home."

Elise and I looked at each other. Home was Montgomery. Home was our house and our school and our friends and our dog. It was the clothes in our closets and my sister's boyfriends and the neighborhood where we rode our bikes down the middle of the street because there were hardly any cars.

"You mean Alabama?" Elise said.

"He means heaven," I said, reaching for the breadbasket and knocking over my glass in the process. The wine spilled all over the white tablecloth, pooled in my plate.

"Nice job," Elise said.

"Jess," my father said, like I'd ruined everything, like everything had been going so well up till now. He got angry when I spilled things, when I swallowed water too fast and it went down the wrong way. It was like he thought I did these things on purpose.

The busboy took my plate away and brought a towel, sopped it up, but there was still red everywhere, terrible as blood.

My father opened his menu. "Order anything you want."

"Can I ask you a question?" Elise said. Nothing good ever came after that. It was never *How would you like a bowl of ice cream?* Or *There's a good movie playing. Why don't we all go see it?*

"What's that?" he asked.

"How are we paying for this trip?"

"With the money we saved for this purpose," he said.

"We know you lost your job," she said, and I recalled a dinner, much like this one, after our father had gotten that job: white tablecloths and oversized menus, *Order anything you want.*

"I can order the lobster?" I asked.

"Your father said you can order whatever you want," my mother said.

"Have you been leaving the house in the morning and going to the park?" Elise asked. "Or the library?"

I couldn't remember him with a briefcase at all.

"I need you to leave this table," he said. "And I don't want to see your face for the rest of the night." He said "face" in a really nasty way, like it was the most horrible thing ever.

"And don't you leave your room," my mother said. "I'm gonna be up there to check on you in half an hour."

My sister finished her wine and put her hands on the edge of the table like she was going to push. Then she stood and left as the waiter was walking over to take our order. He stood there smiling and we were all so tense I could feel how awkward we were making him. He shifted his weight from one foot to the other, asked if he should come back in a minute. Something about it was satisfying—he wasn't a part of us, didn't belong. We were unhappy together, miserable even, but it was ours.

"No, we're ready," my father said. Then he looked at my mother and asked what she wanted. She ordered the surf and turf with a salad and a loaded baked potato, and the rest of us followed suit.

I imagined my father at the kitchen table a few weeks from now opening the credit card bill, the smell of pot roast we'd be eating for days. My mother would have us bag up all our old clothes for the Ultcheys and the other families who had given their money away, as if they needed our worn-out clothes, while my father assured them that we would all be in heaven soon, that this was not the life He had intended for us. I wondered whether he really believed it, if he'd ever believed.

The busboy brought another basket of bread and my father tore off a piece. He spread a thick layer of butter on it and immediately dropped it on his shirt.

"Seems like I can't hardly eat without getting something on me," he said, dipping his napkin into his ice water. I watched as he rubbed his shirt until a large wet spot stuck to his chest.

When the salads came, we stabbed at the pieces of lettuce. I drank the little bit of wine in my glass and didn't ask for more. After a while, my mother attempted to make pleasant conversation but neither my father nor I were interested. It must have been the quietest meal of my life. My father didn't even pray when the steaks and lobster tails were placed before us.

After dinner, I pulled my mother aside and asked if I could

get Brother Jessie's number. I'd prepared an answer but she didn't ask, just got out her phone and called it out to me.

———

When I got back to the room, Elise wasn't there. There was a note on the desk: "Meet me at the Irish bar. You can wear my blue dress."

I sat on the bed, staring at Brother Jessie's number. Though I saw him twice a week at church, and sometimes on Saturday mornings for breakfast in our kitchen, I'd never had any reason to call him. It made me nervous, talking on the phone to people I wasn't used to talking on the phone to.

I hit the call button. On the second ring, he answered.

"Brother Jessie?" I said. "This is Jess Metcalf."

"Jess," he said, "it's so good to hear from you. How are you?"

"I'm good."

"That's good to hear," he said. His voice sounded different. People always sounded different on the phone; they used their phone voices. "So tell me, what's happening?"

"We're in Arizona. Somewhere around Phoenix, I think."

He made some affirmative-sounding noises so I said other stuff—how it felt like we'd been driving for a very long time, how things weren't going very well. I told him about the car accident, the flat tire. He said car trips were like that, accidents and flat tires, that those things weren't out of the ordinary.

"It was a really bad accident," I said. "A man died. I touched his neck, trying to feel for a pulse."

"I'm sorry," he said.

"And there was a little girl. I think she was in a coma." I felt like crying, but if I started, it might go on forever. I'd cry for Tammy and the bird woman and the Las Vegas girl, for my mother and father and the baby Elise wouldn't have and my cousin who had died before she'd figured out how to live.

"We're all praying for y'all," he said. "The whole congregation."

"Thank you."

"What you're doing is a good thing."

"Thank you," I said again. And then, "How come? Why is it a good thing?"

He took a swallow of whatever he was drinking, ice clinking in his glass. "You're spreading the word," he said.

"We haven't been spreading the word that much."

"I'm sure you're doing what you can."

"No," I said. "We've hardly talked to anyone."

"Maybe your father thinks it's best for you to concentrate on each other right now."

"I don't know what we're doing. I feel kind of lost," I said. I wanted to tell him everything, wanted him to say I was okay, that we were okay, but he wouldn't. He'd be disappointed. He might be angry.

"It sounds like you're about to make a breakthrough," he said, the ice clinking again.

"It does?"

"Jess, forget about your family and the trip for a minute. Have you prepared yourself for Him?"

"That's why I'm calling, I don't feel prepared at all. I don't even know if I want it to happen."

He paused for a moment, as if to let this sink in, and said, "What if it's not Him you're doubting, but yourself?"

That sounded right. I had no reason to trust myself.

"There's something you're not telling me," he said, and his baby, Rachel, started crying. She had some kind of deformity, one side of her face pocked with strawberries, a tumor eating up her eye. A benign tumor, my mother said, not life-threatening or even painful, though I didn't know how she would know whether it was painful or not. The only time I'd held her, I put my hand over the bad side of her face to see what she would have looked like normal, what she was supposed to look like. She would have been a pretty baby.

His phone fell to the floor and he picked it up. "I'm sorry," he said. "You still there?"

"I'm here." I turned on the TV and pressed mute—no matter what station you left it on, it defaulted to the hotel's channel. At the spa, a smiling brunette was giving a pretty Asian woman a facial. I wondered if they hired actors or if these were real employees.

"Tell me," he said.

"Tell you what?"

"Tell me."

"I don't know what you want me to say."

"How you violate yourself," he whispered.

"What?"

"Do you want to be forgiven?" His voice cracked on the word "forgiven." "We all want to be forgiven, Jess." He breathed my name into the phone—*Jess, Jess*—as I sat there, unable to say anything. We were quiet for a long time, maybe ten seconds, and then he said my name louder, more clearly. I threw the phone across the room; it hit the wall and bounced off. I walked over and picked it up, knowing I hadn't thrown it hard enough to break it. It made me hate myself. I was always worried about everything, how much a new phone would cost, how much trouble it would be to go to Verizon and get a new one. I wanted to break it and not think twice about breaking it. I wanted to be beautiful enough to demand expensive things and believe I was worthy of them.

I made a half-assed search through Elise's suitcase for a cigarette, but of course she had them with her. Then I went to the bathroom and sorted through her makeup bag, the inside coated with a thick film of shimmery powder. I put on eyeliner, mascara, and blush. I used the hair dryer and some lotion to try to get my hair to do something it didn't want to do. Then I put on Elise's blue silk dress, a dress I'd specifically asked to wear before and she'd said no, and stood in front of the mirror. I didn't look like a different person, but I didn't quite look like the same one, either.

———

The bar was like Applebee's with its green-glowing beer signs, men hunched over baskets of fried food. Elise was seated at a four-top by the window with a salad in front of her, watching a tennis game on TV. She'd changed into a new outfit, a short black dress and a pair of heels. She might pass for a woman meeting friends for drinks after work.

"Order a Coke," she said. "I have a flask."

"Where'd you get a flask?"

"Dan gave it to me for my birthday." She took it out of her purse and passed it across the table. GET YOUR SHIT TOGETHER, it said. "The whiskey I got at the liquor store. It cost me twenty dollars of your money."

"Oh yeah?"

"That's right," she said. "You won't need it where you're going."

"I wish you'd stop taking my money," I said.

"That's the first time I've ever taken your money."

"I wish you'd stop asking for it, then."

The waitress came and I ordered a Diet Coke. I looked around—it was Friday night and people were celebrating the start of their weekend. Weekends meant nothing to us. We had no reason to keep track of days except for the one our lives had been revolving around for months.

My drink came. I took a few gulps and poured the whiskey in. I stopped myself from checking to see if anyone was watching. If someone saw us, they might say we couldn't do that, or kick us out. I told myself it didn't matter—worst-case scenario, we got kicked out and we'd go someplace else, but even though the worst-case scenario wasn't even bad, I dreaded it. I hated to be told I couldn't do something. I checked my breasts, adjusted them.

"How are your boobs?" she asked.

"Nice."

"You look pretty."

"Thanks."

We drank for a few minutes and then she said, "I've been thinking about something."

"What's that?"

"Cinderella's slipper."

"Cinderella's slipper," I repeated.

"Yeah—how come it didn't turn into a rat or whatever when the clock struck twelve?"

"Why would you be thinking about that?" I asked.

"Because I was thinking about leaving my clothes outside and it reminded me." She took out her cigarettes and her LOVE HURTS lighter and placed them on the table, though there were no ashtrays and no one was smoking. "It's a good question, right?"

I wondered if she'd just light up, like a movie star. "I don't know. I haven't seen *Cinderella* in a long time."

"But you know the story."

"Yeah, I know the story."

"The slipper's left on the step and the prince takes it around—"

"I know what happens," I said. "Have you seen the boys?"

"No," she said. She took her straw out of her glass and drank from it, tiny little sips like she was feeding an injured baby bird.

"I called Brother Jessie," I said.

"Yeah? What'd he say?"

"He asked me to tell him how I violated myself."

"He asked you to tell him *what*?"

"He said, 'Tell me how you violate yourself.'"

"Bullshit," she said.

"No, I'm serious. I could hear his baby crying in the background. Rachel."

"Stop."

"And the ice clinking in his glass." I picked up my Diet Coke and moved it around but there was too much ice, the glass too tall and thick.

"What are you gonna do?"

"What do you mean 'what am I gonna do?'"

"I mean 'what are you gonna do?'" she said.

"Nothing."

"What are you talking about? What if he's done this to other kids? What if he's done a lot worse?"

Who cares about other kids? I thought, but then I felt bad. I cared about other kids. "I doubt he's done anything," I said. The one and only time he'd touched me, we were at church. I'd been sick and hadn't seen him in a few weeks and he'd pulled me to him, cradled my head to his chest. The hug had gone on too long—anyone who'd seen the entire thing, gauged its length, would have found it inappropriate.

"We have to tell Dad," she said.

"Why? We never tell him anything."

"But this is important," she said, looking at the door. I turned to watch the guys from the pool walk over. There were four of them, sunburned and wearing their nice clothes.

"Can we sit?" the one who'd held me asked.

"Sure," I said. His eyes were bloodshot, a swampy green.

Two of them went to get chairs and the other two sat, making a lot of noise and taking up as much space as possible. They seemed wrong out of water.

The fattest, loudest one put his hand on the back of my chair and smiled with all of his teeth. The one who'd held me—Jay or Jason—picked a cherry tomato off Elise's salad and popped it into his mouth. She pushed it across the table to him and took out her flask, poured more whiskey into her glass. I wondered if she was always so standoffish, or if she only acted this way for my benefit. Who was she, really? Was she the person who rode bikes with me and jumped on the trampoline, or a careless drunk who went off with strange men and did God-knows-what? Was she a standoffish bitch, or a good-hearted person who was kind to the most downtrodden of God's flock?

"What's your name again?" I asked.

"Jake," he said.

"Jake," I said. "I like that name."

"You guys been here long?" the fat one asked.

One of the others set shots on the table. "Date grapes for everyone," he said.

"That's not funny," I said.

"That's what they're called. We all got date grapes, not just you guys. I'll get you a birthday cake next if you want."

"I'll have a birthday cake," Elise said.

We held up our shots.

"To new friends," the guy who'd bought them said.

"To the rapture," said Elise.

We clinked glasses and drank. I drank half and set the other half back down. I could feel my blood start to move again. I couldn't hear the buzz in my ears, but if I went to the bathroom I might be able to hear it.

"I'm Brad," the guy who'd bought the shots said.

"Jess."

"You're a bad cheerser," he said, and asked if he could give me a lesson. He picked up my glass of Diet Coke and whiskey and gestured for me to raise my shot. "First you make brief but meaningful eye contact." We made eye contact that was longer than brief. I smiled, but he looked at me like this was serious business. "Then you raise your glass, clink, and look the person in the eye again. And *then* you drink. If it's a shot, you take the entire thing—not half."

"I can drink half if I want to," I said.

"You can," he said, "but that's not how it works."

He had me practice until he was satisfied I'd gotten it right. Then he took out his wallet and went back to the bar. I wanted to know a man well enough to go through his wallet. I imagined faded, unused, and expired things, a stack of warm bills. Everything mine for the taking.

The fat one started telling me about Yelapa, Mexico, a place he'd lived after he graduated high school. He'd made a lot of money crabbing and spent his free time surfing. He'd go back there one day, he said. He'd live on a boat and sail somewhere when he got bored and eat fish right out of the ocean. I tried to make eye contact with Elise but she was talking to Jake, laughing and touching her hair. It was getting so long, like Amish hair. Like Mennonite hair. He told me about a particular tree where he'd always find coconuts that had sprouted, the inside like a marshmallow you could eat with a spoon. But sometimes they'd sprouted and were bad.

"How could you tell if they were bad?" I asked.

"The smell," he said, shaking his head. "The smell was awful."

I didn't care about him or his dreams, but it didn't stop me from imagining the two of us on a boat, scooping the marshmallows out of coconuts before they turned.

"So Jess called our pastor earlier," Elise said, and everyone stopped talking and looked at me.

"Elise," I said.

"And he wanted to know about her masturbation techniques."

"He wanted to know what?" they said. "Wait up, hold on a second."

"Tell them," she said.

I told them the story: the phone call, the ugly baby, ice clinking in his glass. As I talked, I realized how infrequently I told stories to a group. I didn't like feeling that I had to hold their attention, like at any second I could lose it. This was a good story, though, and they sat with their elbows on the table, leaning in. When I was finished, I had the same conversation with them that I'd had with Elise, about what I was going to do. I didn't like this talk about what I was going to do. I would tell Shannon and my mother, maybe, and she could tell my father if she thought it was necessary. But there was something else that made me want to keep quiet—I didn't want anyone to say I was lying. I'd only told the story twice, and was sure it had happened, but already it felt like something I'd made up.

"That's some fucked-up shit," Brad said after everyone had returned to their separate conversations. I took a sip of my drink. He said he was sorry that that had happened to me. There was an awkward pause and then he tapped the window. "I'm in asphalt," he said, still tapping, as if I didn't know what asphalt was.

"It must be boring being a grown-up," I said.

"There are perks."

"Like what?"

"Like I can walk into any bar and have a drink."

"I'm having a drink at a bar right now and I'm fifteen."

"You're having to be careful, though," he said.

"I like being careful," I said, which wasn't true. I was tired of being careful. Kids weren't supposed to be careful all the time. I wanted to be like my sister, who made friends and mistakes easily. It was like she'd been born knowing how to live.

———

Half an hour later, the boys left to go to a different bar and Elise and I walked over to the coffee shop. I bought a brownie and we sat at the bar facing the casino floor. I looked around for my father.

"Do you want some?" I asked. The brownie was huge, like a giant piece of birthday cake.

"No," she said.

"It's terrible, like a grocery-store brownie. Really waxy." I squashed a corner into the doily, getting chocolate in my nails. This made me happy and I smiled and then looked around to see if anyone had seen me. I didn't like to be caught entertaining myself in public; there was something humiliating about it, though I couldn't say what it was.

The woman on the other side of me had a mug of tea. She held it up to her lips and blew. Tea looked so relaxing. I thought I should start drinking tea.

"Hello," she said. She was in her mid-twenties, with a boy haircut and long dangly earrings. She asked where we were from.

"Alabama," I said.

"Alabama the beautiful," she said.

"That's right."

"Is it beautiful there?"

"It's okay."

"Is it green?"

"It's pretty green," I said, "but not like some places, not like North Georgia or anything. It's just regular green."

"I miss green," she said.

Elise jumped off her stool and said she'd be back, and the woman and I were quiet, watching people move around the floor. There were a lot of old and disabled people, but there were plenty of young people, too—girls in dresses and sandals, boys in khaki shorts and collared shirts. They looked so easy, relaxed. I wondered how many of them felt that way.

"Why are you here?" the woman asked, moving her head so her earrings swung back and forth.

"We're staying at the hotel," I said, "me and my parents and sister. My dad likes to gamble."

She waited for me to say more, but I didn't. Then she said,

"I'm with my family, too. Last summer we stayed at a cabin at Slide Rock and this summer . . ." She waved her hands around. "I guess I don't always get to pick."

"How many nights are you here for?" I asked.

"Just two. I told them I couldn't stay any longer than that." She took a sip of tea. "I brought along some projects to occupy myself, but I don't see myself doing any work. This isn't exactly a work-conducive environment."

"No," I said, my eyes following a long-haired boy in smiley-face pajama pants. I folded the doily around the rest of the brownie and squeezed until oil soaked through. "What do you do?"

"I'm a caregiver," she said. "I sit with elderly people."

"Oh, that's nice."

"I guess. It leaves me a lot of energy to make my art."

"What kind of art?"

"All kinds—photography, murals. I work a lot with found objects."

"Oh wow," I said.

"And sometimes I write things."

"What do you write about?"

"Last week I wrote a twenty-word poem about honor killings," she said. "Do you know what honor killings are?"

"Like when a woman in the Middle East cheats on her husband and her family has to get their honor back?"

She nodded. "It was titled 'Field's Last Bloom.'" She continued nodding and I wondered if she nodded so much when she wasn't wearing dangly earrings. She must have liked to feel them move. "After I finished writing it, I felt compelled to do something so I found an empty field and dug up the words by hand."

"Really?"

"Yeah."

"Wow," I said. "That's really neat. Whose land was it?"

"I don't know."

"You don't know?"

She shook her head, took another sip of tea.

"How'd you get the letters to look the same?" I asked.

"I didn't bother too much with that," she said.

"Was it hard?"

"The hardest part was remembering which letter I was on. I kept having to go back and check."

"That's really neat," I said again.

She shrugged and drank her tea. I wanted to know why she'd done it, what the point of it had been, but I didn't want to offend her. It seemed unbelievable that someone would spend so much time and effort doing something so purposeless. It would have been better to donate money, or write a blog post about it. I imagined her standing in front of the poem after it was complete and seeing nothing but a bunch of holes. Like a pack of moles had dug up the ground.

"Did you take any pictures of it?" I asked.

"A few, but only for myself."

"That's really cool. I'd like to do something like that."

"You should," she said. "I'll do anything once and if I don't like it or I'm not having fun, I'll think, *You are having an experience.*"

"So you're thinking that right now?"

She smiled. "Touché."

I'd never met anyone like her. Instead of watching TV or playing on the Internet, she wrote poems about human rights issues and searched out empty fields. It made me envious, but I also felt sorry for her. If she went back there now, her words would be unreadable; she'd have nothing to show for her efforts. But maybe that was the point.

———

Elise returned with a plastic bag and I stood and told the woman it had been nice talking to her.

"You too," she said.

"I hope you get to go camping next year."

"Thanks," she said, and then she wished me luck. I didn't like it when people wished me luck. It was like they thought I needed it, like I wouldn't be okay without it.

On our way out of the coffee shop, I saw my father. He stopped at a machine and stared at it for a moment, pressed a few buttons. Then he sat at the one beside it. I wondered if someone would come along and sit next to him, at the machine he knew he should be playing, and hit it big. I wondered if he always chose the machine right next to the one he felt compelled to play, if he always purposefully fucked himself.

Elise tripped, nearly falling on her face. I took the bag out of her hand and looped my arm through hers.

"How'd you get so drunk?"

"I'm not that drunk. I just need to eat something," she said. "I got me some french fries."

I slowed as we passed the Native American store with its turquoise jewelry and dreamcatchers, watching the girl behind the counter. She had long silky hair but she was wide-faced and flat-nosed and thick.

"Hold on a second," I said to Elise, and signaled for her to sit on a nearby bench. I stepped into the store and smiled in the direction of the girl, who remained slouched over the counter with her hands folded in front of her. "How much are the dreamcatchers?" I asked.

"All prices," she said. "I think our least expensive one is sixteen."

"I want it," I said.

"It's that one," the girl said, nodding to one in a corner.

"I want it," I said again. It was perfect, the one I would have chosen even if I hadn't known the price.

She stood on a stool to get it down for me. She wasn't that big but her butt was disproportionately large and I wondered why she didn't do something about it, go on a diet or do some kind of target exercises.

"What do they do?" I asked. "I mean, how do they work?"

"Positive dreams slip through the hole in the center and glide down the feathers to the sleeping person," she said, like she'd said it a hundred times. "The negative dreams get caught up in the web here. Do you have a lot of bad dreams?"

"I don't know," I said. "I don't know what a normal amount of bad dreams are."

"I never have bad dreams."

"I dream my teeth are falling out sometimes."

"You're worried you're not attractive enough," she said. "Or you're sexually frustrated, but they all seem to mean that."

This irritated me. I was a lot better-looking than she was—nine out of ten boys would pick me over her, or at least eight.

"I'm really into dream interpretation," she said. "Give me another and I'll tell you what it means."

"I don't remember any others," I said.

"Come on."

"Sometimes I dream I find a treasure chest and it's full of gold."

"Hmm," she said, twisting up her mouth. "You're about to unlock some important information that you've kept hidden from yourself. Of course it could mean other things, too. I'd need to check my book."

This made me wonder if I'd been molested as a child and had repressed it. When people unlocked important information, wasn't this always the case? Nobody ever unlocked anything good. I handed her my money, hooked a finger through the loop, and didn't thank her as I walked out. This went against everything I'd been taught and felt very liberating.

Elise was still on the bench. "A dreamcatcher," she said, putting her cigarette out on the floor.

I explained how it worked, that the bad dreams got caught up in the web and the good ones slipped down the feathers.

She stuck a finger in the hole and wagged it. "My dreams have been all fucked up lately," she said. "Like they're picking up where somebody's left off the night before."

————

An elevator was open and we stepped inside—we had it all to ourselves. I looked at myself in the mirror, first one and then turning to look in another and another. One day I would have a house without mirrors, not a single mirror to remind me of myself. It was amazing to think about, having my own place where I could do whatever I wanted. I could go to bars and drink beer or watch *Friends* reruns in bed for days and nobody would be there to say anything. I could order pizza and answer the door in my pajamas. When the elevator was about to stop, I jumped so I could feel the floor rise to meet me.

At our room, Elise couldn't find her key. She emptied her purse all over the carpet, shaking it and turning out the fabric lining.

"What are you doing? I have one right here."

The woman across the hall opened her door and deposited another room service tray outside. She was in a white bathrobe, pink foam curlers in her hair. She closed the door and Elise crawled over and picked up a perfect half of an untouched sandwich. "It's got turkey on it," she said, tossing it down the hall.

"Go pick that up," I said, gathering her stuff, running my hands over the carpet to make sure I'd gotten all of her bobby pins and loose change. I noticed the chocolate in my nails, like dirt.

"Do you want to see the birds?" she asked. "Let's go see the birds."

"She's probably asleep."

"I want them to land in my hair." She flipped over onto her back with her legs and arms splayed, lightly touching her head with one hand.

"Get up."

"You look funny from this angle," she said, laughing. I left her there and went into our room, set her food and purse on the bed. I laid the dreamcatcher on my bag and looked at it. I hardly ever bought anything for myself, and never anything so decorative. I couldn't wait to get home and find the perfect place to hang it. The light on the telephone was blinking red—a message from our mother.

I went to get Elise but she was already in the bird woman's room.

"Come on in and close the door," the woman said. She was in bed in her big purple dress, Luke in a cot by the window, shirtless.

Elise opened the middle cage, and I went over and knelt next to her. The birds stayed where they were, one on either side, their heads tucked into their bodies.

"I think they're asleep," she said.

"We were all asleep," Luke said.

"What if they see the other birds?" I asked. "I thought they'd beat their wings and go berserk."

"They will," Luke said.

"It'll be okay," the woman said.

"Come here, little birdies," Elise said. "Pretty little birdies, sweet little birds." She called to them like she was calling a dog, patting her knees. I could feel Luke's eyes on us. We probably reminded him of all of the girls who'd never liked him—girls who'd made fun of him in elementary school and then hadn't cared enough to do even that. Elise called louder.

"Just be quiet for a minute," I said, taking her hand. We backed away from the cage and waited. I glanced at Luke in his cot with its thin white blanket. He hadn't bothered to cover himself, and his breasts—they could only be called breasts—were small and folded over. They were different from a woman's, missing whatever was inside them that gave them shape.

Finally, a bird flew out and perched on the fat woman's foot. It looked around with its jerky bird neck before flying from one wall to the other as if measuring the dimensions of the room.

"This one likes to peck," the woman said. "Not hard, just little love pecks." The bird flew back to her foot and demonstrated, and the woman squealed and tossed her head about.

"I want it to peck me," Elise said.

And then the other bird was out of its cage and they were both flying, stopping to look at us from the desk, the top of the TV cabinet. It reminded me of being a little kid, how I'd stand on tables and chairs to see things differently. How it would alter my perspective in the most pleasant way. I leaned against the wall and watched them. At the beginning of summer, on a walk around the neighborhood with Cole, a baby bird fell from its nest and landed at our feet. I'd nearly stepped on it. I was sure it had been some kind of omen, like a black cat in a dark alley, only a thousand times worse. It was dead, slick and eyeless.

When I looked at Luke, his eyes moved off to the side. He was the kind of guy who walked into a library or a movie theater and shot up a bunch of strangers, the kind who wouldn't even have the guts to shoot himself afterward. He'd put the gun in his mouth and pull it out, put it in and pull it out, and then maybe break down in tears.

No matter how she called them, or how still and patiently she waited, the birds wouldn't go near Elise. She stood and held out her arms like a scarecrow and they cut an even wider arc around her.

———

We got in bed and opened the box of fries, drenched and soggy with cheese.

"This is the orangest cheese I've ever seen," I said. I stuck a finger into a corner, cold and gloppy.

"That means it has a lot of nutrients," she said.

Or it's poisonous, I thought. "Mom called," I said. "We should call her back."

"You call her."

"She called my cell, too. She's probably freaking out."

"So call the woman."

We ate while watching Anderson Cooper, our dresses wrinkled and hiked up our thighs. She stopped eating to tell me about Anderson's brother, how he'd committed suicide. "'I can't feel anything anymore,' he said, hanging from the ledge of a tall building. And then he let go." She said he was handsome and rich and had everything and he still wanted to die.

"Do you want to die?" I asked.

"*No*," she said. "I love my life."

"Are you being serious?"

"Yeah, why wouldn't I be?"

"I thought that was your point." I concentrated on getting as much cheese onto each fry as possible before putting it in my mouth. "How do you know Anderson's gay?" I asked.

"He's thin and well-groomed and eats a plain baked potato for every meal."

"A plain baked potato?"

"That's what I read. He thinks eating is a burden."

"I wish I was like that," I said. I closed the box and threw it away, washed the cheese off my fingers. Then I took off Elise's dress and hung it in the closet, put my shorts and tank top on.

Anderson was over and some other guy was talking about the rapture. If the rapture was supposed to start at 10 P.M. tomorrow night in California, it would start earlier in other parts of the world. For some reason this hadn't occurred to me. Australia was waiting to see what would happen. They were sixteen hours ahead of us and it would all begin, or not begin, in a few short hours.

"Shit," I said. "I forgot." It seems like God wouldn't care about time zones. Why do we have time zones again?"

"Because people used to set their time based on the sun but

it was a mess," she said. "Imagine if you were traveling and had to catch a train or something."

"How do you know everything?"

"I make stuff up a lot," she said. "People don't question it if you act like you know what you're talking about."

"I'm not going to be able to sleep now," I said. "I'm going to have to stay up all night and watch."

"You can sleep with the TV on," she said, nuzzling my arm.

———

There was a knock at the door, a series of hard raps. Elise ran over and looked out the peephole. "What do you think? Should we let them in?"

They heard her and called yes.

"What about your boyfriend?" I asked.

"I don't have a boyfriend."

"Yes you do."

"I think I'd know it if I had a boyfriend," she said.

They knocked again, calling our names, and she opened the door. They walked in like they belonged, but when they got to the middle of the room, stood there looking out of place. And then one of them sat in the chair and another sat on the bed. One of them said he had to take a piss and went to the bathroom. The last one looked out the window and commented on the view.

The one who'd bought us date grapes, Brad, was on the bed.

"Make yourself at home," I said.

"I will, thanks," he said, taking off his shoes. He had a nice

smile, much nicer than Gabe's, but I wanted Gabe, my beautiful boy. My beautiful, lovely blond boy. Why hadn't he texted
me? I hoped he didn't think I was just some girl who had given
him a handjob in the back of his van. I was, of course, but I
couldn't think of myself that way, and couldn't think of him
thinking of me that way, either. There had been something special between us.

Brad ruffled my hair. I had the urge to go to the bathroom
and check, but I just smoothed it back into place and looked at
my sister, standing on the bed. She ordered the Yelapa guy to
stand in front of her and climbed onto his shoulders. Then she
directed him around the room, running her hands along the
bumpy ceiling. She told him to jump and he hopped, his feet not
even leaving the ground.

Brad played music on his phone, a tinny, desperate sound, as
Jake took a tin of cigarettes from his shirtfront pocket. He pulled
out a wooden box and slid the top off.

"What's that?" I asked.

"Weed," he said.

"You can't smoke that in here, people will smell it."

They said everyone was asleep but us, that no one would
smell it. They said they'd been smoking in hotel rooms for years.
I imagined the police kicking down the door and arresting us,
taking us to jail. Our father would have to come down to the
station and bail us out, and he'd be disappointed in me.

"Light it up," Elise said.

They passed the little metal cigarette around: inhaling,
coughing.

"I might want to try it," I said.

"I thought it was a gateway drug," Elise said.

"It's a slippery slope," Brad said, passing it to Jake. Jake knocked it against the table and refilled it, handed it to me. I held a lighter to the end and the weed burned as I sucked. I didn't feel like I was getting much, but I breathed out a huge puff of smoke.

"I don't think I feel anything," I said, after a while.

"It's pretty shitty weed," Jake said.

"I didn't feel anything my first time, either," Elise said. "Or I was so drunk I couldn't tell if I felt anything."

I took another hit, sucking and sucking and breathing out a ton of smoke. I coughed—it felt like the smoke was trapped in my throat and I couldn't get it out.

"That's enough for you," Elise said.

They continued passing it around while I watched TV. The reporter was interviewing people on the streets, asking them whether they believed the rapture was coming. I didn't know why reporters were always interviewing people on the streets. I had a thought about it, something that seemed like a very good thought, but then someone said something and I lost it and couldn't get it back. I didn't even bother trying because I knew it was no use.

"Hey, Jess," Elise said. *"Jess?"*

"What?"

"You're grinding your teeth."

"I'm not grinding my teeth," I said, unclenching my jaw. I was also digging my fingers into my legs. I stood and took my phone into the bathroom, stared at Gabe's number. I typed things and deleted them, typed and deleted. He didn't love me. I wasn't special. I went back out and resumed my place on the floor.

I didn't like the way the weed made me feel, so I took another hit, hoping it would make me feel differently.

————

"Come on," Brad said, taking my hand and leading me to the bathroom. He locked the door behind us. His face looked larger and redder in the bathroom light and I didn't want to be alone with him but I also felt special, chosen.

"Hi," I said, as he moved toward me.

He propped me up on the counter and put his hands on my thighs. They felt a lot like my own, hardly like anything.

"Hi," I said again.

"That was your first time smoking?" he asked.

"Yeah."

"How'd you like it?"

"Fine," I said. "I don't care about anything."

He tilted my neck and kissed it, held my hair back with one hand. He was pulling too hard but I didn't say anything. "I want to make you feel good," he said. "Can I make you feel good?" He kissed me before I could answer, his hands moving higher and higher until they were touching my panties, rubbing the thin material between two fingers. I couldn't remember which pair I had on. They were probably a good pair because the good ones weren't as comfortable so I saved them for last. I wondered why Elise hadn't knocked. The old Elise would have knocked already, would have come looking for me last night.

"Are those veneers?" I asked, pulling away.

"No," he said.

"They're perfect, like movie star teeth."

"Close your eyes."

"You must not drink any coffee," I said.

"I drink plenty of coffee," he said, "and I smoke, too." He sounded angry about it. I closed my eyes and he tilted my neck and kissed it again. Then he began to suck and I wondered if I was going to wake up with a hickey; the thought of it excited me.

In the room, a Bruce Springsteen song played, one I didn't know.

Brad unbuttoned my shorts, tugged at them.

"It bothers me that Bruce Springsteen is always talking about factories and being poor. Once you've got that much money you shouldn't be able to write about being poor anymore," I said.

"This was only his second album," he said. "He wasn't rich then."

"He was a rock star, though."

"Shhh."

"Don't tell me to shhh. I don't have to be quiet."

"No," he said. "We can talk about Bruce if you want."

"That's all I wanted to say about it." I lifted up and he pulled off my shorts. I was wearing a pair of blue panties that had lace at the top in a lighter blue, one of my prettier pair that fit well and didn't have any bloodstains.

"These are sexy," he said, running his finger along the lace. Then he moved them to the side and pushed his finger in, first one and then two. He said I was tight and I hoped he didn't say anything else about it. I smiled at him. My smile felt big and fake and made me think nobody could ever love me.

He unbuttoned his shorts, unzipped them, and pulled himself out—half-hard, big.

"It's big," I said.

"Is it?"

"It seems really big."

"It's not huge or anything," he said. He took out his wallet and found a gold condom. I watched him open the wrapper with his teeth, roll it down his dick.

"Wait," I said, placing my hands against his chest.

"What?"

"I don't know."

"We don't have to," he said.

"No," I said.

"I'll go slow." He gave me a sad look like he might love me, pulled me forward, and pushed himself in. I didn't want to do it anymore and wanted to stop him—all I had to say was that I'd changed my mind. I could just pull my shorts up and leave the bathroom and he would let me. I could leave. I didn't have to do this. I scooted to the edge of the counter and wrapped my legs around his waist.

"Hey," I said, but it was so quiet. I put my hands under his shirt and held onto him, tried to concentrate on his skin, which was smooth and warm. I wanted to pull him on top of me, wanted him to smother me, make it hard to breathe.

After a few minutes, he grunted and tugged my hair. Then he was still and silent. I tried to move but he held my legs in place, closed his eyes. The bluish lids were lined with veins. There was a tiny mole below his left eye that added so much.

He peeled the condom off, hobbled a few feet over to the toilet, and flushed. Then he put his hand on the back of my head and smiled at me before zipping his pants.

When he left, I locked the door and set about cleaning myself with a washcloth. I peed, brushed my teeth, washed my face. When there was nothing left to clean, I sat on the toilet and listened to them talk and laugh, knowing I would never be a part of it. I would always be separate, thinking about what expression my face was making, what people thought of me. Observing peoples' weaknesses and flaws—their big thighs and crooked teeth and acne, their lack of confidence, their fear. I would always think the worst about people and it would keep me from them because I couldn't accept myself.

———

Elise sat alone on the bed, wobbling back and forth. I got up and went to the bathroom, peed for the fourth time in two hours.

When I came out, she was fumbling around in the closet.

"What are you doing?" I asked, sliding open the door.

"I have to use the bathroom."

"You're in the closet," I said. I turned on the light and led her to the toilet, stood there until she told me to go away. I got in bed and tried to get comfortable. I imagined myself melting into the mattress, becoming a part of it.

A few minutes later, she came out unwrapping something.

"What do you have?" I asked.

"A candy," she said, popping it into her mouth.

"You might choke." I held out my hand and she spit the peppermint into it. I set it on the table and told her to go to sleep, but she began to cry, softly at first and then gasping, sucking breaths that hurt my chest, my heart.

"Elise?" I said. "Hey. What's wrong?"

"You know what," she said.

"It's okay."

"It's not okay."

I wanted to list things, like our mother listed things when our father lost another job, or when we didn't have enough money to go back-to-school shopping. She would remind us of all the things we had—our health and each other and a roof over our heads—things we'd always had so they never seemed like anything. I could tell her she was beautiful and smart and funny and popular, that she could walk into any room and heads would turn. But I didn't say these things and the crying slowed and I thought it would stop but it started up again, terrible and heaving. I wondered how anyone would ever be able to love her. She was too beautiful. It was like being too rich—all you could think about was what the person could do for you.

I walked over to the tub and turned on the pitifully slow-filling faucet. I could still feel Brad inside me and wondered how long it would take to go away. *I hate myself*, I thought. I thought it again and again and it felt good, like I was finally admitting something I'd kept secret for a long time.

"Why don't you take a bath?" I asked, watching the water creep into the tub.

She didn't say anything. I sat there for a moment, looking at her, and then took off my clothes and got in, waited for the water to fill up around me. I ducked my head under and held my breath, my ring scraping the porcelain—God was supposed to be my husband. I was supposed to be married to God. I imagined slicing my wrists open, red against white. It would be so bright, so beautiful. I could hear my heartbeat and remembered that it only had so many. It seemed cruel, putting a little bomb inside us like this, something that we had to always find new ways to ignore.

I adjusted the water with my foot and looked over at my sister.

"What's the worst thing you've ever done?" she asked.

"Worst like what? The meanest?"

"Whatever."

"I used to like Marc," I said. "Do you remember Marc?"

"He only carpooled with us for like four years," she said.

"I couldn't talk to him so instead of being nice I was really mean. I put gum in his hair and told him he smelled bad and one time I told Mom he'd gotten another ride home and we left him in the rain."

"I remember that—we had to go back and get him and he was soaked."

"And now he's in Ohio and I'll never see him again," I said. "He'll always think I hated him."

"I bet he knows you liked him," she said. "Kids do shit like that when they like each other."

"I don't think so."

"Maybe he didn't know then, but I bet he knows now."

"I hope so," I said.

She was quiet and I wanted to ask about the worst thing she'd ever done but she'd probably done some actual bad things, which was why she was asking. She turned onto her side, facing away from me.

"I love you," I said.

"I love you, too," she mumbled.

"I'm sad we're not going to make it to California. I wanted to see the ocean."

"I'm sure it's not that great."

"I bet it's nice."

"These aren't the last days of California," she said. "You'll see it eventually."

A few minutes later, she was asleep. No matter what, she never had any trouble sleeping.

I got out of the tub and dried off with a damp towel. I let it fall to the floor and walked over to the window, stepped onto the ledge. The blue light of the parking garage reminded me of a mosquito zapper. It could have been dusk or dawn. I pressed my hands to the glass and leaned forward, thinking about Brother Jessie's baby. Why would God have given him a baby like that? I wondered if his wife had spent her pregnancy afraid, if it had caused the baby to be deformed. If I ever became pregnant, I'd be terrified the whole time, and my baby would be born dead or worse, completely messed up. I'd have no choice but to sacrifice my life for it, and people would say how good I was, how selfless.

I closed the curtains. Then I put on my clothes and got in bed, letting my hair soak the pillow. At home, I'd have waited for it to dry, or put a towel down. At home, I wouldn't drop things when I was done using them. I checked my phone. As usual, no one had called or texted. Before I could think better of it, I typed a message to Gabe—*I've been thinking about the back of your van*—and pressed send. Then I set the phone screen-side-down on my chest and waited. A minute later, I picked it up and looked at it, adjusted the volume. He was probably asleep. It was late and he was asleep and had been asleep for hours, but I needed him to be awake. I wanted to tell him everything. I felt like he would understand, that he was the only person who would understand.

I played games with myself—counting down from ten, ignoring the phone—but nothing worked, so I gave up and recited the Lord's Prayer. I said it over and over until the words got all mixed up and I had no idea how it went.

When I finally fell asleep, I dreamed I was blind except for a small square in the upper right-hand corner of my vision. I had to keep moving my head around, positioning the square in just the right place so I could see. I saw a banana, reached out and grabbed it. I peeled it and took a bite and each bite brought back more and more vision until I could see normally. Then I dreamed we were at home and my mother was in the driveway, being dragged off by a snake as big as a car. My sister yelled for me to get our father so I went inside and found him asleep in his chair. *Gunsmoke* was on TV, which made it feel less dreamlike. Instead of screaming, I shook him until he woke up and we ran outside, but by that time, the snake had her whole body in its mouth and we just stood there and watched.

SATURDAY

When I woke up, Elise was curled around me. I scooted away from her and checked my phone. Gabe had responded at seven forty-eight: *Hey girl. What have you been thinking about it, exactly?* I didn't know what to write back. I wanted to be flirty, yet serious. I wanted to be serious, mostly, but I'd started it by being flirty. I was happy he'd written back, but it also seemed like too little too late. He couldn't help me.

I turned on the TV. There had been no reports of Christians gone missing. Marshall was unavailable for comment. We were going to have to drive back to Montgomery, but I didn't want to go back to Montgomery, or I didn't feel like driving anymore, ever. I wondered if we could stay in Arizona. I imagined myself beautiful in Arizona—my hair longer and fuller, my skin clearer. My mother could get a teaching job and my father could find work in a place where people didn't know about all of the jobs he'd lost. Where he could start fresh. And Elise could have her baby, or not, and no one would give a shit. I thought of other reasons, ways I might try to sell them on it, while I watched my sister sleep.

After a while, I went to the bathroom—my stomach was queasy and I had a dull headache, but I looked better than I ever had in my life—cheeks and lips flushed, eyes burning. My dirty hair looked darker, nearly thick. I studied my pores in the magnified mirror, the light making halos in my eyes.

I turned on the little TV and sat on the toilet. It was a show I'd seen before, the people pretending it was the 1800s. They were on a farm with pigs and chickens and the women were sweating in ankle-length, long-sleeved dresses. A butch woman washed clothes while a more attractive woman made biscuits. You had sex, I thought. *You did it.* I wanted to feel more, for it to hurt, so I kept repeating it to myself. *You had sex. You aren't a virgin anymore.* I called myself a slut and a whore while digging my nails into my thighs to move the feeling from my chest to my legs.

———

An hour later, we were in our parents' room, lounging in their empty tub while our mother talked to one of her sisters. She'd given us dirty looks when she'd opened the door but hadn't said anything about not calling her back. She didn't want to get off the phone.

"I have no idea where we are," she said. "We could be in Toocumterry for all I know." Toocumterry was her version of Bumfuck Egypt. She was wearing the dress we called her carpool dress; it was green and blue tie-dye, old and soft. Elise and I were wearing the tank tops we'd slept in. We had our sunglasses on, hair piled on top of our heads with bobby pins. Along with my slight hangover, this ensemble made me feel cool and jaded.

I hooked my arms over the back of the tub and watched the muted TV, the nonevent unfolding across the globe. The rapture hadn't happened in China or Russia. It hadn't happened in Japan or Vietnam or India or Cambodia. Somewhere in Australia, a group of drunken revelers released helium balloons with blow-up dolls attached.

"Australians are so weird," Elise said.

"You've never even met an Australian," I said.

"You don't know."

"Who?"

The toilet flushed and our father came out of the bathroom, still in his robe. He paused before taking a seat at the edge of the bed. "That was some bill y'all racked up at the pool yesterday," he said. He took off his glasses and held the bridge of his nose. "Room service, too. Hot fudge sundaes—everybody likes a hot fudge sundae."

Elise raised her sunglasses to look at me.

"We didn't think you'd have to pay for it," I said.

"No," he said. "Of course you didn't." He didn't say anything else, and we listened to our mother tell one of her sisters about the fabulous dinner we'd had last night—it was the best lobster she'd ever put in her mouth. The lobsters had been small and overcooked, but our steaks had been good—tender, medium-rare.

My father turned the sound on, a reporter interviewing an unknown man. The man said we were likely to go through the

stages of grief from denial to depression. He said we would probably experience psychological trauma and may consider suicide.
I looked at my father to gauge his reaction.

I climbed out of the tub and sat next to him. "Are you okay?"

"I'm okay," he said. Then he patted my leg and said I was his
girl and I loved him so much in that moment. I was his girl and
would always be his girl.

"It could still happen," I said.

"No it couldn't," Elise said.

"The Middle East is full of Muslims," I said.

"Australia's mostly Christian. New Zealand, too."

Now that she told me she made things up, I was suspicious
of everything. I got out my phone and Googled "Drunken revelers in Australia release blow-up dolls," but there was no sign of
these people. Most of the links had to do with women and binge
drinking.

My father walked over to the window. "Why don't y'all go
back to your room for a minute and let me talk to your mother,"
he said. But we'd left our keys in our room; our bags were in
their entryway. Elise pointed this out and asked if he wanted us
to go to the coffee shop.

I went to the bathroom and admired my face some more, my
red lips. I was thirsty but didn't feel like drinking any water.

"Jess," Elise called. "What are you doing in there?"

"Nothing."

"Will you make me some coffee?"

I sorted through the little plastic bin. "There's only decaf."

"Go find the lady."

"Go find her yourself," I said. I went to the door and looked out. There was a cart in the hall. I walked over and saw a cleaning lady pushing a vacuum by the window. I tried to get her attention but she didn't see me so I opened a plastic drawer and took out two packets. Just as I was turning, she met my eye—a flash of hatred and surprise.

I ran back to the room like someone was chasing me and tossed them to my sister.

"It would taste better if you made it," she said.

I got in the tub and we watched coverage we'd already seen—dozens of news vans camped outside of Marshall's offices, a wide lot and a half-dozen trailers. A pretty black woman in a pantsuit knocked on a door. No one answered, so she knocked on another and another until she was back at the first one. It was always so damning when no one could be reached for comment. Then it cut to a reporter interviewing a man from the Florida leg. He was in the driver's seat of a rapture van, his tan arm hanging out the window. The reporter asked if it had been a waste of his time and the man said he had brought many people to God, that lives were changed because of what they'd done. I looked at my father and wondered if he could convince himself he had changed lives. He didn't look sad or traumatized or angry. He didn't look anything.

"I hope they show Greta," Elise said.

"I don't," I said.

"Why not?"

"I just don't." I imagined the door to her home ajar, all of her electronics gone. Cats gone, husband. The faces of her plain, overweight children stapled to telephone poles. Long after they were found dead, strangers would still be peering into their eyes.

My father stood and wheeled his suitcase into the bathroom. "We have to be out in forty-five minutes," he said.

Elise and I looked at our mother, who was now watching something on her phone.

"She hates us," Elise said.

"Don't say 'hate,'" our mother said, glancing up at us.

"See? She hates us." She took the bobby pins out of her hair one by one and laid them on the edge of the tub.

"I always wanted two girls—two girls, two years apart. You know that."

"I'm sure you were so specific," Elise said.

"We're two and a half years apart," I said.

Elise put her feet on either side of my head and lifted herself into a backbend, her crotch pointed at my face. She moved her head from side to side and her hair swung back and forth like a pendulum.

On our mother's phone, a crowd cheered.

"What are you watching?" I asked.

She turned the screen to me but I was too far away. "Have you seen this video?" she asked. "This man in Oregon made a video proposal."

"No. Why would I have seen it?"

The cheering died down and a man was telling a woman he loved her more than life itself. Then he was saying he was going to spend the rest of his days trying to make her happy. He didn't say anything remotely original and the woman, of course, was crying.

When the boy I loved proposed, he wouldn't say the usual things about how much he loved me or get on one knee. He'd say he wanted to die with me in a freak submarine explosion. He'd say he loved me down to the squishy insides of his bones. I could help him come up with things if he needed me to. Boys had trouble expressing themselves because they weren't as good with language.

Elise walked over to the desk and picked up the landline.

"What are you doing?" our mother asked.

She turned her back to us and placed an order for room service, more food than we could eat. It was probably going to cost a hundred dollars.

I looked at my mother, smiling at her phone. I wanted to go to her, curl up in her arms. I missed her and wanted to tell her I missed her. At home, we shared bowls of popcorn, sat close to each other on the couch to watch movies. When we were finished eating, we'd scratch each other's backs. *I want to put you in my pocket,* she'd say, *so I can pull you out whenever I want.* I would imagine myself small, pocket-sized, nestled against the warmth of her leg. I was afraid she would die without knowing how much I loved her, and it made me want to tell her things, let her get to know me, but I didn't think she'd be able to love me if she knew me.

———

Our father came out of the bathroom smelling like Colgate and Barbasol, same as always. He sat on the bed and opened his Bible.

"You won last night, didn't you?" Elise said.

He grinned, the kind of grin we only saw when he returned from the casino with a wallet full of money. That hadn't happened in a long time. I couldn't remember the last time it had happened.

"How much?" I asked.

He raised his eyebrows at us, and his hand moved to his wallet as if to check and make sure it was still there.

"Did you get your picture taken?" I asked.

Years ago, when he first started gambling, he'd won big. He was given balloons and an oversized check and had his picture taken; the photo was hidden in his underwear drawer. Winning was the worst thing that had ever happened to him, he'd said once, in a rare moment of reflection.

"Don't give them any of it back," Elise said.

"I'm not going to," he said, "don't worry," and then he began to read as if it were any other morning, only he started at the beginning: "'*The earth was without form and void, and darkness was upon the face of the deep; and the Spirit of God was moving over the face of the waters.*'"

I closed my eyes and listened, trying to picture the earth without form, the water with a face. I thought I could see the water's face. It was happy. Elise got up and went to the bathroom. Our father kept reading: God rested, man took his first breath, God planted a garden.

My phone beeped. I hoped it was Gabe, but it was Elise: *Come in here.*

She let me in and sat on the floor, pressed her knees to her chest. "I think I'm having a miscarriage," she said.

"How come?"

"Because I'm bleeding a lot and it hurts really bad." She looked at me like I'd know what to do, but I didn't know what to do. I caught my eye in the mirror.

"Maybe we should go to the hospital," I said.

"No."

"Maybe you're just spotting. I've heard that happens."

Our father raised his voice. "'*Then the man said, This at last is bone of my bones and flesh of my flesh; she shall be called Woman, because she was taken out of Man.*'"

"It hurts so bad," she said. "Do you think you could go get me some ibuprofen?"

"Did you check to see if she has any?" I asked, sorting through our mother's makeup bag: POND'S Cold Cream, Q-tips, thick pads wrapped in pink and green, a tube of brownish lipstick in the shade she'd worn forever.

"I saw it," she said, "it was a big clot of blood. Clottier than the usual clots."

I stood there for a moment, looking down at her, and said I'd be back. Then I closed the door and slipped on my flip-flops, thinking about the baby in the toilet, a big clot of blood.

"Elise is sick," I said, interrupting my father, who was coming to the part where the woman screws everything up, bringing curses upon the ground, turning everybody to dirt.

"What's wrong?"

"She has a stomachache."

He took out his wallet and handed me a bunch of ones, said he thought we'd already bought Pepto-Bismol.

————

At the sundries shop, the only medicine came in envelopes with two to a package. I counted the money my father had given me—seven dollars—and then counted my own—thirteen. I wanted to spend it all, felt the need to get down to zero. There was no one else in the store so I started setting things on the counter: three packages of Advil, a Diet Coke, a big bag of peanut M&M's, which were Elise's favorite, and an *OK!* magazine with Kristen Stewart and Robert Pattinson on the cover. I took the elevator back up, walking faster as I neared our room. I didn't know how to feel about what was happening. On the one hand, it would be over, everything fixed. On the other hand—I wasn't sure, exactly, what was on the other hand, but I knew there was something. And maybe she wasn't having a miscarriage at all. What did she know about having a miscarriage?

I knocked and my mother answered. "Is everything okay?" she asked, leaning in. I wondered if she could smell alcohol on me. "Elise said she only wanted you."

"She just has cramps."

"Oh," she said, her eyes searching my face. She stepped back and opened the door wider. She knew Elise didn't have her period; she was the one who was always running out to buy tampons and pads and panty liners, Midol and ibuprofen. Among the three of us, we couldn't keep these things in the house. My period came at the tail end of my mother's, would be starting any day now, at any moment, but Elise's wasn't due for another two weeks. I wasn't sure why I had said this and wished I hadn't.

Elise opened the door to the bathroom and I handed her the medicine; she ripped open a couple of packets and swallowed the pills. "It knew I didn't want it," she said. "It could feel it."

"It's not your fault," I said, though I didn't know if it was her fault or not. Maybe the baby *had* known, maybe it had felt everything she felt. I thought of Rachel, with her half-hideous, half-normal face, and fingered my ring, running it back and forth along the chain so it made a nice zip noise.

We sat on the floor and watched TV. It was nighttime and the women were in a circle, sewing by candlelight. One woman was talking about dropping out of the project, saying she didn't know why she'd signed up for it in the first place, what the point of it was, while the others tried to talk her out of it. The more they tried to explain the purpose of the experiment, though, the less sure they sounded. And then they were all talking themselves out of it—they were hungry and hot and might even go blind. Didn't the girl from *Little House on the Prairie* go blind, like for real, in real life?

"Are you okay?" I asked.

"I'm fine," she said, looking at me so miserably I felt like I'd lost something, too. It could be terrible having a family—you had to suffer their pains and disappointments along with your own—but the good stuff couldn't be shared, at least not in the same way.

"Maybe it's not a miscarriage. Maybe it's just a little blood."

"I know my body," she said.

I know my body, I thought. *I know my body.* I wanted to know my body. We ate M&M's and watched commercials for cleaning products and lunch meat, and then it was morning and the women were back at work, feeding the animals and washing clothes and there was no more talk of abandoning the project. Elise sorted the M&Ms by color; she ate the red ones and the brown ones and the blue ones in twos and threes. I bit into one that didn't have a peanut, which was lucky, like finding a four-leaf clover in a field.

When we'd finished the bag, I took her hand and held it. I held it until both of our hands were sweaty and I wanted to let go but didn't. I wanted her to know I would always be there for her, that I would never leave her.

"I have to change this pad," she said finally, and I stood and closed the door behind me.

————

As soon as Elise came out, the food arrived—plates of scrambled eggs and bacon, fruit salad, pancakes, a carafe of coffee.

"Are you feeling better?" our mother asked.

"A little," she said. She sat on the bed with us and I reached out and touched her hair. She smiled at me and poured herself a cup of coffee, stirred in cream and a packet of sugar. She put a spoonful of eggs on her plate, a scoop of fruit salad.

Our father popped the needle out of his case and pinched his belly, but stopped before shoving it in. "I think I'm going to go on that hospital diet Woo's been trying to get me on," he said.

"That's a great idea," our mother said, handing me a roll of silverware.

"I could do it," he said.

"Of course you could."

"You don't think I could do it," he said.

"You can do anything you put your mind to," she said in a cheerful voice that confirmed his suspicions.

"I think you can do it," I said.

"I do, too," Elise said. "You're the most stubborn man we know."

He chuckled and pushed the needle in, saying perhaps it would be one of the last times he'd have to stick himself. Then he bowed his head. "Thank you, Lord," he said. "These are simple words but they come from simple hearts that overflow with the realization of your goodness. We ask you to bless us as we eat, bless this food and bless the hands that prepared it. May the words of our lips spring forth from hearts of gratitude and may we bless others as we fellowship today." He paused and we waited for him to say something else, something more. "Thank you for our family," he said. There was another pause and he said, "Amen."

"Thank you for our family," our mother repeated.

I put a single pancake on my plate, a piece of bacon.

Elise turned it to *The Price Is Right* and we watched while we ate. In the Showcase Showdown, a woman won a trip around the world. Her friends rushed the stage and they ran around looking at the pictures of the places she would go. It was better when they all got to pile in a car and wave through the windows. They might actually get to cruise around in that car but they weren't going around the world. I thought about the dusty flea market with the saddest lady I'd ever seen, the camel in the parking lot of the dollar store, the old man pushing his lawnmower across the highway. They were all things I wouldn't have seen in Montgomery. I wondered if the Las Vegas girl made it to Las Vegas. I hoped she had and that her life would be better there. I imagined she'd kept the dog, calling to him at the last minute.

And then *The Young and the Restless* was on and I asked questions, trying to catch up with who was with who, what was happening. We were finished eating but no one moved. Once we moved, we'd have to keep moving. We'd have to get in our car and drive home and that would feel like failure but it didn't feel like failure now. It felt like all sorts of things were still possible.

"Are you going to eat that?" I asked my mother.

She handed me her last piece of bacon, soft and floppy like all restaurant bacon.

"Give me half," Elise said.

I gave her the whole thing and she ate it like she'd never stopped eating meat. And just like that, she wasn't a vegetarian anymore. It was strange how you could be something and then not be that something so easily. Last night, I'd been a virgin.

Elise had been a vegetarian. Last night, not being those things had seemed impossible. I eyed the remaining biscuit, an unopened jar of jelly. I picked up the jar and peeled off the thin black strip that said it hadn't been tampered with, took a clean spoon and held it up to my face.

ACKNOWLEDGMENTS

I am indebted to the Michener Center for Writers. It was my dream to be a Michener Fellow and I still can't quite believe it came true. Thanks to my professors, Michael Adams and Elizabeth McCracken, who were incredibly generous with their time and expertise. I couldn't have done it without you. A number of friends also read early drafts: Melissa Ginsburg, Ethel Rohan, Elizabeth Ellen, Aaron Burch, Derek Asuan-O'Brien, Dolores Ulmer, Nick Ulmer, Claudia Smith, Jane Collins, and Lee Durkee. Thank you. Thank you, Katie Adams, for taking a chance. Lastly, thanks to Sarah Bridgins, who wanted to represent a woman who said she would always and only be a short story writer.

ABOUT THE AUTHOR

Mary Miller is the author of the story collection *Big World*. Her work has appeared in *McSweeney's Quarterly*, *New Stories from the South*, *Oxford American*, and *American Short Fiction*. A former Michener Fellow in Fiction at the University of Texas, she will serve as the John and Renée Grisham Writer-in-Residence at the University of Mississippi for the academic year 2014–15.